F
WEAVER

HARD BALL

Also by Will Weaver

Striking Out

Farm Team

HARD BALL

A
Billy Baggs Novel

by
Will Weaver

HarperCollins*Publishers*

Library of Congress Cataloging-in-Publication Data
Weaver, Will.
    Hard ball / by Will Weaver
      p.   cm.
    Summary: A fourteen-year-old Minnesota farm boy has to figure out how to get
along with the arch-rival in his love life and on the baseball diamond, and both boys
must learn how to deal with the unfair expectations of their fathers.
    ISBN 0-06-027122-1 (lib. bdg.). — ISBN 0-06-027121-3
    [1. Baseball—Fiction.   2. Fathers and sons—Fiction.   3. Competition
(Psychology)—Fiction.   4. Farm life—Minnesota—Fiction.   5. Minnesota—Fiction.]
I. Title.
PZ7.W3623Har   1998   97-26597
[Fic]—dc21   CIP
                                                                         AC

                    1   2   3   4   5   6   7   8   9   10
                                    ❖
                             First Edition

For Bruce and Linda Johnson,
friends in deed

Prologue

That summer in northern Minnesota, word spread. In Flint County there was a young baseball player, a pitcher, like few people had seen. On the mound he was a fireballer. A speed demon. Had a rocket launcher for an arm. The kid was a farm boy, that much was certain. He also had his own team, a motley crew that was unbeaten because no one had ever laid a bat on the boy's fastball.

So who was this phenom? Some said he was a stocky sixteen-year-old who could fire a baseball through a barn wall and leave only a charred smell. Others said he was a lanky fifteen-year-old right-hander who threw so hard that the ball sent out a silent whistle that set dogs to howling a full mile away. Still others said he was a seventeen-year-old left-hander who could throw the ball so high that a player could step off the field, take a pee, zip up and get back in position before the ball hit dirt; one old man swore he'd seen the ball come down a full five minutes later, shining and glazed with ice.

So much for gossip. In truth the boy's name was William Jefferson Baggs—Billy Baggs—and he was a fourteen-year-old left-handed farm boy from western Flint County, which lies not far from the headwaters of the Mississippi River. Billy was six feet tall and rising, and had yellow hair, blue eyes and buck teeth, plus a spattering of pimples across his cheeks. He was skinny but square-framed, and his arms, corded and stretched from farmwork, were his chief weapons.

And yes, his Farm Team was unbeaten. They had edged the local Flint Babe Ruth team and its ace pitcher, Archer "King" Kenwood. They had hammered the nearby Buckman town team. They had spanked various 4-H, Grange and church clubs that had dared bring a team to the Baggses' farm baseball field. Was Billy Baggs unhittable? Of course not. No pitcher is. There had been three scratch singles off Billy in about forty innings.

Farm Team baseball began that summer of 1971 when fliers appeared in the Flint Feedmill, in the drugstores, in the hardware stores, in the soda fountains and gas stations. "BASEBALL!" they read. "Friday nights (weather permitting) at the Abner Baggs Farm . . . Come one, come all. . . ." These were the years of the Vietnam War, of civil rights unrest and sit-down strikes; however, the people of Flint were mostly untouched by all that, and they hoped to remain that way. All the more reason, then, to take in a country-style ball game.

So they came. Young ballplayers from around the county. Bored vacationers stuck at nearby resorts. Friendly farmers and townsfolk with nothing better to do after supper. A college coach or two in the Flint lakes area for fishing. They all came to sit on hay-bale bleachers and watch Billy Baggs fire his white-hot heater past batter after batter. Following each game at least one coach lingered and introduced himself to Billy, who, with a brief handshake, was polite enough but had faraway eyes. After every Farm Team game Billy scanned the crowd for a tall girl with a silvery ponytail. Her name was Suzy Langen, and Billy was in love.

One small problem. Suzy already had a boyfriend, the same one since kindergarten. His name? King Kenwood.

1

August 1971

Billy couldn't sleep. The August night heat, trapped in the attic of the farmhouse, kept him turning in his sheets. That and Suzy Langen, the judge's daughter, who was never far out of his mind these days. Unfortunately, with thoughts of Suzy came King Kenwood, who was never far from Suzy's side.

He lay there, imagining ways to get rid of Kenwood once and for all on tomorrow's trip. A stumble beneath the school bus tires? An accidental fall from the window at sixty miles an hour? Then again, Billy would be the prime suspect, and he didn't need more trouble with the law this summer. He squinted shut his eyes and brought back Suzy. Suzy tall and smiling, her legs and arms coppery brown against her white shorts and blouse. Suzy at the beach in town, slowly milking river water from her long hair. . . .

Just when he felt drowsy, a huge August moon began to glow brightly in his window. He got up and yanked down his shade. After that he lay there, watching the moonlight leak in. By four thirty A.M. he gave up on sleep. He dressed in jeans and a T-shirt, and eased down the stairs to the porch, where he put on his coveralls. Quietly latching the screen door, he crossed the farmyard under the still-bright moon.

Inside the dairy barn he flipped on the lights. "If I can't sleep, neither can you," he announced. The big Holstein cows huffed through their noses and jangled their stanchion chains. They began, one by one, to tip themselves upright, white on black, black on white, until they stood like dominoes in two even rows. Rousted a full hour early, the cows were as cross as Billy. However, they soon snaked their long tongues at the buckets full of grain Billy splashed their way. He was all done with feeding and had started milking by the time his father arrived.

"Well ain't you the early bird," Abner said from the doorway. He was a tall, lanky man, as dark as Billy was fair, with a dusty seed cap drawn low across his forehead and a limp from having polio as a kid.

"Sorry, Pa. Couldn't sleep." The air compressor motor for the milking machine kept up a quick, steady thudding sound—a sound, suddenly, like Billy's heartbeat. He was always slightly afraid of his father. Afraid that he was doing the wrong thing. Afraid that he was doing the right thing.

"You know what?" Abner muttered as he took over the stainless steel milker.

"What's that, Pa?" he asked quickly.

"I'll be damned glad when this Minneapolis trip of yours has come and gone."

Billy was silent. He supposed he had been distracted the past few days. One thing he had not forgotten to do was cross off the days on his calendar. Or check the time.

"Don't worry, you ain't gonna miss that bus," Abner said.

"I wasn't worried," Billy replied.

"Then why do you keep looking at your watch every thirty seconds?"

"Sometimes it stops," Billy mumbled, and headed to feed the calves. He sneaked yet another glance at the time.

In the house at breakfast Billy made sure to chew his pancakes slowly to prove that he was in no hurry.

"Well, a big day," Mavis said cheerfully. His mother was the optimist in the family.

Both Billy and Abner glanced at each other.

"Big day of work on the farm, for me," Abner said. "I've got to get the silage chopper tuned up, plus there's some fencing to be done and—"

"And nothing that can't wait," Mavis replied. "Sometimes it's important to take a day off."

"Tell that to the dairy cows," Abner replied, reaching for another hotcake.

"Lighten up a little," Mavis said easily to Abner. She was a tall, handsome, square-shouldered woman with brown hair tied back. She tended to point things—in this case her pancake turner—at people when she talked. "This is Billy's day to have some fun. He's been home, working, every day of the summer—no thanks to you know who."

Billy held his breath. During Abner's stay in jail his mother had claimed some kind of territory, some kind of power in the family. Now that his father was back, she made a point of not giving it up. Billy, who had run the farm this summer, had felt that power, too; however, now that Abner was home, Billy felt his turf eroding, his independence slipping away. He held his breath a lot when his father was nearby.

"Being in the slammer was sure no vacation, if that's what you're saying," Abner growled.

"Of course it wasn't," Mavis said cheerfully. "But I'm saying that it's behind us now and we're glad to have you back. And today is Billy's day to get away and see a ball game. Like a normal kid," she added.

Billy hated it when she said that.

"Hmmmph," Abner muttered, eyeballing Billy briefly before bending to his pancakes. "I guess I'll have to listen to the game on the radio."

"We'll go together next time!" Billy said suddenly. "All three of us. I'll check out where the stadium is, what roads to take, and then next time we all could go."

"I'd love to see the Twin Cities sometime," Mavis began.

"Not me," Abner said. "The traffic in Fargo is bad enough."

———

The three of them rode to town in Abner's pickup. Mavis had had her own car, a Chevy, but it had been the source of their recent troubles. Abner, angry at Mavis for buying a used car without consulting him—and then madder still at Randy Meyers, the car salesman who had sold her a lemon but would not refund the money—had taken his D–6 Caterpillar to town. To make a long story short, Randy Meyers A-1 Cars, which they were approaching on the left, had looked like the site of a B-52 air strike in Vietnam. Only Meyers's sign remained upright, its multicolored banner flapping in the breeze above the hulks of crushed cars. Billy had been there that day with his father, trying to talk him out of it—but both had gotten in trouble: Abner sixty days in jail plus two years' probation, Billy a rap sheet and a social worker, no thanks to County Attorney Mark Kenwood.

"Not a word," Mavis warned, as they drew even with the site of their summer's misfortune.

"Did I say anything?" Abner said. He slowed the truck to look, with no small pleasure, at the destruction.

"You were thinking of saying something," Mavis said.

Billy took a long look at his parents. Some kids had doctors and lawyers for their parents, some kids had judges and scientists, some kids had teachers and writers; he had Abner and Mavis. Parents were the luck of the draw. Sometimes he wasn't sure whether he had gotten low cards or high ones.

"What are you staring at?" Abner said, feeling Billy's gaze.

"Nothing," Billy said.

Abner slowed for the green city-limits sign—FLINT: POPULATION 2001—then turned toward the school. "Now don't forget your lunch," Mavis said to Billy, rustling the large sack of fried chicken and homemade bread.

"It's not like I'm going to be gone for a week," Billy said.

Ahead, in the raw early sunlight, the school bus gleamed like a monstrous state-fair squash. Crawling about it, like ants at ground level, were dozens of kids, mostly ninth-graders-to-be. Their parents were milling around, fussing with coolers and sacks of gear. A few were farm kids, including the shaggy-haired McGinty brothers, who stood to the side holding bag lunches like Billy's. But most were town kids, laughing and loud, bareheaded and wearing fashionable summer clothes. Billy surveyed their shorts, their bright shirts and blouses. He was wearing his new Twins cap, bought especially for this trip by Mavis, plus a black T-shirt and blue jeans, ironed with sharp creases. There was nothing he could do about his ironed jeans, but he ditched his cap.

A long white Cadillac pulled in behind the Baggses' pickup. Abner lifted a dark eyebrow toward his mirror. "Well, well. If it isn't our friendly county attorney, Mark Kenwood."

Mavis turned. "He's only dropping off his boy, just like us," she said.

"Nothing about that family is like us," Abner replied.

King Kenwood got out of the passenger side. He wore sunglasses, a white polo-type shirt, khaki shorts, and leather boat shoes, no socks. Billy always felt shabby beside him, especially holding a paper sack containing most of a dead chicken.

King Kenwood, carrying nothing, went toward a group of his town friends. His father followed; their path took them near the Baggses' truck. "Hey there, Billy Baggs," King said by way of greeting. It was calculated to annoy, his always using Billy's first and last names.

"Hello, 'Arthur,'" Billy answered; he knew King hated jokes about his first name.

King look at the old pickup. "I didn't expect you'd be on this trip."

"Why not?" Billy said.

"I thought farm kids had to work all the time. Make corn when the sun shines, something like that." A couple of his friends snickered.

"Billy's taking the day off, like a normal kid," Mavis said from her window.

Billy let out a sharp, exasperated noise. King grinned at his embarrassment.

"It must be nice having your father home," Mark Kenwood said to Billy. Broad and dark like King, he wore a tie and his usual smile, which never quite reached his eyes. King's father also had a way of looking Billy up and down—at his arms, his legs, the size of his feet—then glancing at his own son as if he was comparing two workhorses.

"You want to talk to somebody in my family, talk to me," Abner said to Mark Kenwood. The pickup's door squeaked sharply as Abner got out.

"Come on, Dad," King said, and moved his father along.

"Just trying to pass the time of day," Mark Kenwood said.

"Pass it with somebody else," Abner said.

A shiny station wagon pulled up beside the Kenwoods' Cadillac. Several girls from Billy's grade got out.

"Billy, who's the one with the silver ponytail?" Mavis asked, happy to change the subject.

Billy froze. It was Suzy Langen. She had on white shorts, her tanned legs shone in the sunlight and the long, soft rope of her hair swayed from side to side.

"I dunno," Billy said. He was suddenly occupied with gathering his stuff.

"She's been coming to some of our Farm Team games this summer," Mavis added. She narrowed her eyes and glanced toward Billy.

"Oh, her?" Billy said, looking up briefly. "That must be . . . ah . . . Suzy."

"Suzy who?" his mother persisted.

"Well, I guess I've got everything," Billy said.

"I can tell you her last name," Abner said suddenly. Billy's eyes widened as Judge Langen himself got out of the driver's seat of the station wagon. "It's Langen. That damn Judge Langen himself."

"Don't," Mavis said quickly, putting a hand on Abner's arm. "Not now."

"Why not now?" Abner said, his eyes fastened on the tall, square-jawed, white-haired judge, who went to speak with King's father. Abner's hands tightened around the wheel. "Judge Langen and Mark Kenwood standing side by side. I ought to accidentally let my foot slip off the clutch and run over the both of them."

"Let it go, Pa," Billy said.

Abner turned his slow steely gaze on Billy. There was a long moment of silence. "What did you say?" Abner said.

"I said to let it go," Billy replied, swallowing, ready to dodge a blow, ready to bolt.

"Let *it* go?" Abner repeated.

Billy looked away; he knew the *it*. The *it* was the deep wound in their family, one that never entirely stopped aching. Robert, Billy's older brother, had died six years ago in a farm accident. Billy had been there, in the field that day, on the tractor with him when it happened. Langen, then county attorney, had seized on their troubles and made an issue of kids and farm safety. Because of the publicity he was eventually elected judge. Mark Kenwood, his assistant, had moved up to county attorney.

"You know what I mean," Billy mumbled.

"He means let it go for today," Mavis said firmly.

Abner slowly returned his gaze to Langen and Kenwood.

"Billy, have you got everything?" Mavis said, seizing the opportunity to change the topic. "Here's your cap. You can't forget your cap."

"I don't want a cap today."

"Maybe he doesn't want to look like a farm kid," Abner said. His eyes were still on Langen. Billy glanced angrily at his father. "I might lose it or something; that's what I meant."

"Okay, fine; you don't have to wear it," Mavis said quickly. Her eyes scanned the other kids, their bare heads, then came back to Billy.

Just then Tiny Tim Loren, a town kid who always homed in on Billy like a pesky deerfly, came running up to the truck. "Hey, Billy! Want to sit with me on the bus?"

"No."

"Billy!" Mavis said. "Be nice."

"Thanks, Mrs. Baggs. I'll go save us a seat!" Tim called, and rushed off.

"Great," Billy said sarcastically. "Just great, Ma."

"It is going to be great. This whole day is going to be great. Now, do you have everything?"

"Yes."

"And are you sure you don't want your cap?"

"I'm sure," Billy said, exasperated. Other kids were staring.

"Then say good-bye to your pa."

" 'Bye, Pa," Billy mumbled.

Abner nodded, ever so slightly, without taking his eyes off Judge Langen.

Mavis got out and walked Billy toward the bus.

Coach Anderson, a hefty, big-armed man in a baseball cap jammed over pepper-and-salt curls, came around the rear. He carried his usual clipboard with the usual forms to sign, and wore his usual whistle around his neck. "Good morning, Billy—and Mrs. Baggs."

"Mavis," she said, smiling. The coach nodded pleasantly. He always had an extra minute for Billy's mom.

"Great day for a trip, Billy," the coach said.

Billy shrugged, though he could not help smiling a little.

"Especially for him," Mavis said. "He'll be the first one in our family to see the big city."

King Kenwood, standing nearby with his pals, turned to stare.

"Imagine that—skyscrapers!" Mavis added, and smoothed Billy's hair again. King's pals smirked.

"Ma, please," Billy whispered. He sometimes wondered if parents practiced ways to embarrass their kids. As Mavis signed off on the coach's clipboard, Suzy Langen came toward the bus carrying a cooler. She was headed his way; Billy swallowed and tried to prepare something clever to say.

King, spotting her in the crowd, called, "Hey, Suzy!" and hurried forward to intercept her.

"Hello, King," Suzy said. She paused, balancing the cooler on a hip.

"My folks are driving down to the game. We've got room in the Cadillac, I mean, if you don't want to ride on the bus," King said.

"Thanks, but probably not," Suzy said easily. "The bus ride is half the fun."

King's dark brown eyes flickered to Billy, then back to Suzy. He could only shrug. "Well, see you down there, I guess," he mumbled.

"Sure, King," she said, and headed out of sight into the bus.

"Tough luck," Billy said softly to King.

King muttered something to Billy.

His mother gave Billy and King a twice-over look, then turned to the coach. "Will you keep an eye on those two?" she said. "They mix about as well as their fathers—on the order of oil and water."

"I've noticed," the coach said wryly. "And believe me, I'll be watching them."

"Be good—and have a good time today," Mavis said to Billy. She gathered him into her long arms and gave him a good-bye hug that lifted him clear off the ground.

"Geez, Ma!" Billy said, as he struggled to get loose. Compared to other mothers, Mavis was a head taller and twice as strong. He always forgot that until she put the clamps on him for a hug.

"And be careful, all right?" she called over her shoulder.

"It's only a baseball game," he called loudly to her, as if he had seen a dozen Twins games. Then, blessedly, Abner and Mavis drove off, and Billy was alone with the long orange bus and the crowd of town kids.

One of King's friends said, "Imagine that—actual skyscrapers!"

Billy dropped his bag. "You guys got something to say to me?"

"Yeah, maybe we do, hayseed!" Doug Nixon said.

Just then Tiny Tim poked his head from a bus window. "Billy! Hey, Billy! I found us the perfect seat."

"I'd check it out if I were you, Billy," the coach said. He had been watching, and he was definitely not smiling.

"Sure," Billy said, shrugging. He gave Kenwood's gang a parting look, retrieved his gear and headed up the scuffed rubber steps.

"Down here, Billy!" Tim called.

He threaded his way to the back.

"Right here," Tim said eagerly.

Billy paused. "I'll sit with you if you don't jabber all the way to Minneapolis."

"Me? Jabber? No way, Billy, no way. By the way, want to see my baseball cards? I brought my entire collection." He held up a long tin box.

Billy sighed and settled in. Outside, the coach blew his whistle and called, "Let's load!" There were excited shouts, and soon feet began to thunder up the steps and pound down the aisle. "No running!" the driver shouted. Bib O'Brien was a fat guy with a beard that came up his cheeks to the bottom of his sunglasses. The students slowed only slightly.

"Watch this," Tim giggled, poking Billy in the ribs as Suzy Langen approached.

"You say anything dumb, and you're out the damn window," Billy said, clamping his big hand on Tim's wrist.

"Oww!" Tim winced. "I may be crazy, but I'm not dumb."

They watched Suzy and another girl, Jennifer, come closer. Suzy glanced up at Billy. "Hi again," she said, smiling.

"Hey," Billy said briefly. He decided it was better to sound uninterested than stupid.

Suzy dropped the rest of her gear onto the seat directly ahead of Billy.

"I planned it," Tim whispered. "You owe me, big time." Then Tim tapped Suzy on the shoulder. "Hey, Suzy, aren't you glad to see me too?"

"Tim, I see quite enough of you around town," she said.

Tim giggled and poked Billy in the ribs once

again. Billy could only stare at Suzy's tanned neck and shoulders, at the way little strands of blond hair hung loose from her ponytail. He breathed in her clean, soapy smell.

Butch Redbird, the Town Team catcher and one of the few Town Team players who had time for Billy, broke the spell. He crashed down into the seat just across the aisle. "Hey, man," he said, panting.

Billy checked his watch. "You almost missed the damn bus."

Butch shrugged. "If I had missed, I'd just stick out my thumb and hitchhike. I could beat the bus to the Twin Cities. Hell, I'd be there waiting for you."

"I doubt that," Suzy said.

"I don't," Billy said. Butch Redbird was from the reservation but lived mostly in town, staying with cousins or friends. He went back and forth anytime he wanted.

"Suzy!" Butch said with mock surprise. "You're on the bus. With the rest of the world."

Suzy turned only her head. "So?"

"So I thought you'd be riding in the Kenwood Caddie."

She shrugged. "Not necessarily."

"A little walk on the wild side, then?" Butch said. "See how the other half rides?"

Suzy let out an annoyed sound and swung her gaze forward. Butch winked at the other boys; he was particularly good at needling her.

Finally the bus lurched forward. With the Kenwoods' Cadillac leading the way, the Twins caravan headed south. Billy watched Flint's Main Street give way to the Feedmill, an auto lot, a propane gas company, the A & W Drive Inn, the weathered Orbit Hi drive-in movie theater, Bud's Junkyard and its long wooden fence decorated with hubcaps—and suddenly they were passing open fields and Christmas tree plantations.

"So," Suzy said, turning to Billy, and making a point of ignoring Butch, "are you going to have any more Farm Team baseball games at your place?"

"Um. I'm not sure. Maybe."

"Town Team should get a rematch," Tiny Tim called, "and no dogs on the roster this time." The reference was to Billy's old black Labrador, Skinner, who played a mean center field; there was laughter all around.

"They were fun," Suzy said. "I'd come again."

"Did you hear that, Billy? She's practically asking you for a date," Butch said.

Irritated, Suzy swiveled immediately to the front. In an instant Billy clamped Butch in a headlock and shook a fist an inch away from his face; Butch, grinning, went limp. "Well, she was, man," he whispered. "It was more the nonverbal signals, the eye contact, the body language."

Suzy looked incredulously back at Butch.

"I read the women's magazines," Butch explained with mock earnestness. "Women communicate differently than men, and it's very important for men to learn their signals. All the articles say so."

"I'm *sure* you read the articles," Suzy scoffed. "It's more likely you're checking out the bathing suits and the lingerie."

"Well, that too," Butch allowed. "For skin, *Cosmopolitan* and *Vogue* are definitely best." There was loud laughter, and the bus rolled on.

Billy frowned. He wished he had Butch's easy way of talking to girls. Instead, he looked out his window, which kept him from staring at the back of Suzy's neck.

At summer's end there were early signs of autumn—an occasional red sumac bush, or an aspen with yellow leaves at the top—but it was the farms along the highway that interested Billy. Most of the farm buildings were constructed of brightly painted metal; on the Baggs farm the outbuildings had wooden slab-board sides and tarpaper roofs. Most of the farms had round, galvanized steel granaries with augers protruding from the bottom; on the Baggs farm the granary was tall, narrow and wooden, with small doors built for a scoop shovel. Most of the farms had automatic manure conveyors poking out the rears of the dairy barns; the Baggs farm used the old method—a fork and wheelbarrow. And most farms he saw had tractors with cabs, or at least roll bars.

Billy thought of his brother, Robert. He stared out his window another long moment, then turned to Tim. "So let's see your baseball cards."

"Really?"

"Sure," Billy said.

Tim unlocked the tin box and began to lay out cards on the seat.

"Some of these old ones belong to my dad," Tim began.

Billy watched Tim as he talked. Tim had intense blue eyes and jerky, twitchy movements. His father and mother were dead, killed in a car crash several years ago. Tim had been injured in the same accident, maybe hit in the head, maybe not; no one was sure. He saw a local psychiatrist once a week and had never yet spoken of his father in the past tense.

"He says they'll be worth big money someday."

"I doubt it," Billy said. He looked down at the faded old cards. Babe Ruth. Lou Gehrig. How would some penny cards ever be worth more than a penny? Especially since the players themselves were long dead.

As Tim chattered on about his cards, Billy wondered what was worse: watching your parents burn to death in a crushed car, or seeing your own brother run over and killed. "Let's see some of your new cards," Billy said abruptly, "like the Twins."

"Twins coming up," Tim said, sorting them expertly. He dealt out a hand of Twins cards onto the worn seat. "Harmon Killebrew. Cesar Tovar. Tony Oliva. Jim Nettles. Rod Carew. Jim Kaat."

Billy read the cards carefully, one by one, losing himself in the numbers, the fine print of minor leagues, of winter ball. The bus rolled ever southward, and the farms and the towns grew larger and brighter.

In Little Falls the Flint caravan stopped at Bye's Café & Filling Station. King Kenwood was waiting by the door for Suzy and cut in ahead of Billy. She had no choice but to sit with King in a booth with all the town kids. Then again, she didn't seem to mind. "Tough luck, Billy," Butch said, grinning.

Billy ignored him and waited for his burger and chocolate malted. He was saving his fried chicken for the ride home.

Afterward they all bought chips and candy for the road. Jake "the Fake" Robertson, wearing an unseasonably heavy jacket, came out of Bye's looking much heftier than when he went in. Back in the bus he opened his coat. Inside it were a pair of new auto floor mats, two quarts of Pennzoil, six Pine Tree air fresheners and a chrome rearview mirror still in its box.

"What a haul!" Butch said.

"A new record," Tim added.

"Bad karma," Butch said.

"Can I have the mirror?" Tim said. "It'd work on my bike."

"Are you kidding?" Jake said to Tim. "It's for Cindy." Cindy was a brown-eyed, well-developed girl, going into eighth grade, who was sitting with Jake. She smiled and fluffed her hair as everyone turned to stare.

"I give them an hour, max," Tim whispered. "She doesn't know how weird Jake really is."

"Jake doesn't know how weird Jake is," Butch added.

Forty minutes later the bus slowed for Saint Cloud, which had some buildings at least a dozen stories tall. "That's Saint Cloud State College," the coach announced. "The tallest buildings are dormitories."

Most of the kids, except the couples in the backseats, turned to look.

"And just ahead is another kind of campus," the coach said.

Tim groaned as if he knew what was coming; he had been on this bus trip before.

"Graystone College, they call it," the coach announced.

Billy stared as high, gray granite walls came into view. They were thick and barn-tall; at each corner was a round turret, like a silo. Inside each of the watchtowers was a man who looked through binoculars down onto the great yard hidden from sight below. Puzzled, Billy squinted at the high walls and the guards. He had heard college was tough, but this was too much.

"Its real name is Saint Cloud State Penitentiary," the coach added.

Billy's face pushed against the window glass. The Pen. Home to Dale Schwartz, the thirty-year-old greaser who had gotten Heather Erickson, the Farm Team's catcher, drunk and pregnant when she was fifteen. Schwartz was another dark cloud on the horizon of Billy's life. Billy had convinced Heather finally to name Schwartz as father of her baby, and Dale had promised to come after Billy when he got out of prison, but that wouldn't be for at least two years. Billy craned his neck as the looming stone walls passed by. In Dale's honor he flashed a middle finger.

"So be sure to eat your vegetables and do your homework," the coach added, "and none of you will end up attending Graystone College."

"I wouldn't be so sure," Cindy said loudly and sarcastically.

Two hours later the skyline of Minneapolis drew Billy's nose to the glass. All the cars, all the buses, all the concrete roads built one over the next; his mouth dropped open. "Wow!"

Butch rapped him on the skull—too late—as Suzy glanced at Billy and smiled.

Billy cleared his throat and tried to look less enthusiastic about seeing the city for the first time.

The bus headed toward Metropolitan Stadium in the southwest suburb of Bloomington. Billy saw other buses from schools across Minnesota, Wisconsin and the two Dakotas. Traffic thickened, slowed to a hobble. On some cars and hippie vans there were flower decals and PEACE NOW bumper stickers. The Kenwoods' Cadillac, caught in a slow lane, appeared briefly alongside and just below the bus, then moved forward again.

The Met Stadium parking lot, with numbered sections, was as wide as a hayfield. There were at least twenty acres of asphalt, most of it covered with cars.

"Section 4-D!" Coach Anderson shouted to everyone. "Remember it."

"Write it on your forehead," the bus driver bellowed. "This bus leaves twenty minutes after the last pitch whether you're here or not. You miss the bus, you're living in the city."

Billy's eyes widened slightly. He scanned the parking lot: northwest corner, 4-D. Home was over two hundred miles away.

"I have your tickets," the coach shouted. "Pick them up from me on your way out."

There was great cheering and bustling and dropping of lunch sacks and clattering of empty pop cans as the Flint kids pressed forward and off the bus. Billy hung back. He watched Suzy Langen's ponytail as she bobbed quickly, confidently through the crowd. Then the throngs of kids streaming off the bus and the thicker knots of people moving toward the stadium gates pulled Billy along. Waves of people flowed into the huge open-air stadium. With any luck King Kenwood would never find the Flint group.

"Beer here!" came the muffled cries from inside.

"All right!" Butch said.

"Don't even think about it," the coach called automatically.

Billy stumbled along, staring at the crowds. A man just ahead of him wore a long ponytail; Billy had never seen a man with hair that long. He had never seen this many people, either, in his whole life. It was like a hundred county fairs crammed into one.

Billy handed over his ticket, got a torn stub in return and followed the rest of the Flint group up a long ramp. Tall wooden bleachers rose up like a forest high overhead, and the sun, glinting through the rickety maze, cast squares and diamonds of light on the walkers. The sunshine grew stronger and stronger as they neared the top. Billy examined the timbers that held up the bleachers. They seemed to be strong enough.

And then Billy stepped out into full view of the stadium—the great open space, with blue sky overhead and the green diamond below.

"Hey, kid! Keep moving!"

"Whatsa matter with you, kid!"

"Get going, kid!"

People jostled Billy as he stood there, mouth open. In the middle of the diamond the pitcher's mound stood like a single pale eye. A pitcher, or maybe a coach, stood behind a low screen and lobbed pitches to the plate.

Crack! A white pinprick of ball soared toward left field. It shone in the sunlight like a white-hot comet.

"Hey, Billy!" Butch shouted. He and Tiny Tim were already several rows above him.

Billy blinked and moved upward.

"We thought you were lost," Tim said.

"Or kidnapped," Butch added, "by women."

Billy kept staring at the field as he settled on the board seat, and his mouth hung open, his buck teeth exposed for the whole world to see.

"Ouch!" someone said in front of him; his knees had banged her back.

Billy looked down. Once again he was seated directly behind Suzy Langen; he tried to recover his wits. "Sorry."

"It's okay," she said, touching her back.

"He didn't mean it; left-handers are naturally clumsy," Butch said.

"Want me to rub where it hurts?" Tim asked Suzy.

She glanced at him disgustedly, then turned back to the field.

Billy balled his fist at Butch and Tim.

"Welcome to today's game/game between the Minnesota Twins/Twins and the Baltimore Orioles/Orioles. . . ." The announcer's voice washed across the stadium. "Please stand/stand for our national anthem/anthem."

Afterward, as the cheering began, Billy joined the noise. When Jim Kaat trotted to the mound, he yelled like crazy and forgot everything except the game.

Left fielder Cesar Tovar, short and dark, trotted past. Harmon Killebrew, big-armed and stubby-legged, took third base below and to the right. The Flint group was seated in short left field, about fifty rows up from the grass.

"This section is great for foul balls," Tim said, slapping his baseball glove. Most other kids and more than a few grown-ups in this section wore their gloves, too. Billy had not thought to bring his glove. It was old and stiff, a wide-fingered cast-off that had belonged to Abner. Looking around at some of the new long gloves that many of the other kids wore, he was suddenly glad he hadn't brought it.

"Co' beer here!" vendor shouted.

Butch raised his hand.

"Forget it, kid," the vendor said without a second glance.

Tim bought a bright pennant, Cracker Jacks and a hot dog before the first pitch, which was a ball.

Billy squinted in the sunlight and wished like hell he had brought along his cap. Jim Kaat reared back with his high, curling leg kick and fired again. Strike! Suzy took out a small set of binoculars. Why hadn't he thought of that? Mavis had a pair of field glasses at home. Everybody around Billy (except Butch Redbird) seemed more prepared. A half thought entered his mind—maybe the other kids were more organized because they didn't have a father like Abner.

"Suzy. Over here!" King called.

They all turned. King waved, then came down the row and knelt beside Suzy. "My father bought some box seat tickets from a scalper. They're only ten rows up from home plate," he murmured. It was clear that he didn't want to be overheard. "There's an extra one if you want it." He showed Suzy a ticket.

"Great! Thank you!" Jake said, leaning forward and snatching the prize.

"Hey!" King said angrily.

Suzy laughed. "Let Jake have it for now. I'll try to drop by later."

Holding his broad back stiffly, King headed back down to the good seats, with Jake following close behind.

"Why do you do that to him?" Jennifer said to Suzy. Her eyes followed King.

"Because he deserves it," Suzy replied. Her eyes remained on the game.

Jennifer looked puzzled, then annoyed. "Sometimes I just don't understand you."

In the bottom of the first inning, with Jim Palmer throwing, the Twins went down in order. Occasionally huge jets passed not far south of the stadium, angling down to the airport. When the big silvery planes thundered overhead, Billy lost track of the game.

Crack! People were making a commotion and jumping up in the section below Billy. Near the grass a ball rocketed foul, glancing off several outstretched gloves, and plopped into the lap of a little girl. She picked up the ball and looked at it, wide-eyed. There was sudden silence; the boys with big baseball gloves stared hopefully at her. Then the little girl tossed the ball back onto the field. There was an instant groan of dismay from the boys, and laughter from the girls.

The game continued, with Kaat mowing down Orioles in the second inning. Billy stared mostly at Suzy Langen. At the side of her face. At the fine downy hairs on her neck.

Suddenly the crowd cheered wildly. The Twins were magically at bat, and Rich Reese was standing on first base as the center fielder tossed in the ball. A base hit, the first of the game—and Billy had missed it entirely! He made himself focus as Leo Cardenas dug in at home plate. His sharp grounder forced Reese at second, and then Jim Nettles came to the plate. After a couple of high fouls, one of which landed only twenty rows down from Billy, Nettles singled to right. "Whoo-ee!" Tiny Tim shouted.

Jim Kaat himself came to the plate. The noise in

the stadium increased. Billy glanced down at Suzy's binoculars. Most of the time she watched the game through them, though once he saw her checking out the Kenwoods' box seats. Billy heard a *crack* and looked up in time to see Kaat stroke a solid single to center, scoring Cardenas.

Billy leaped to his feet and joined the cheering.

"Not bad for a pitcher," Butch said, poking Billy with his elbow. Billy shaded his eyes to squint at Kaat, who was dusting himself off on first base.

"Care for a look?" Suzy said, holding out the glasses.

Billy shrugged. "Maybe later."

In the fourth inning, with Harmon Killebrew at the plate, Billy bent down and picked up the glasses from beside Suzy. Suddenly, up close, Killebrew had a big nose and small eyes; he looked like a million other Midwesterners, like anybody's uncle. Billy was still watching when Killebrew swatted a long line drive. The home crowd went wild, then groaned, as the ball went foul by inches. Suzy Langen's ponytail swayed as she settled back onto the bench. "Did you see it?" she said to Billy.

Billy nodded and handed back the glasses. Their fingers touched briefly. "Thanks."

She looked for a long moment at his forehead, his hair.

"What?" he said.

"I'm not used to seeing you without your cap."

"I'm not used to seeing you at all," he said. Instantly he felt his neck get hot, his cheeks burn; he had no idea what he meant, but she smiled. When she turned again to watch the game, she leaned back against his legs. Butch winked at Billy. After a couple of batters, Billy parted his knees ever so slightly. Gradually Suzy fit herself partway between them.

"Way to go, man!" Butch whispered to Billy.

From then on, oblivious to the game, Billy stared mainly at Suzy. The afternoon heat collected itself in the stadium, and the sun swung high over home plate. The left-field bleachers were a sea of waving programs. Suzy unbuttoned a couple of buttons on her sleeveless blouse and fanned herself. Without trying to Billy could see down a ways, to the white rise of her breasts. He had thought she was slim, way slimmer than what he saw inside her blouse. He forced himself to pay attention to the game, but gradually he began to sweat. It was a new kind of sweat. He felt his armpits begin to run perspiration that even he could smell. In his lunch sack were some paper napkins; during a double-play on the field, when no one was looking at him, he wiped himself dry.

To avoid staring at Suzy, he looked down to the Kenwood box seats. King, with his own set of binoculars, was scanning the Flint group; Kenwood jerked down his glasses.

"Hey Billy, Kaat's up again," Butch said.

"Right," Billy said, and glanced briefly toward the field. After a few pitches he looked at Suzy Langen.

"Not again," Tim groaned.

Billy looked up to see King back in the Flint section. Suzy quickly straightened up.

"Anybody want to sit down front for a while?" King said.

"I do," Jennifer said quickly. She grinned at Suzy as she gave her place to King.

"Tough luck, man!" Butch whispered to Billy.

For the next inning Billy tried to ignore Suzy and King, who talked as they watched the game. But he couldn't help staring at King. At his wide, strong back and shoulders. At his tanned, muscular neck. At the shadow of whiskers down King's cheekbones. King had to shave every day; Billy was lucky to need a razor twice a week. He stared at King's dark-brown shiny hair—the way it hung in perfect, razored layers just to the tops of his ears. Billy's mom cut his hair, or else the local barber, who should have been a butcher. Where in Flint was it possible to get a haircut like King's? How much did a haircut like that cost?

Billy vaguely heard the *pock!* of a bat on a ball, vaguely noticed a swirl of movement around him. The Flint crowd surged to its feet.

"Here it comes!" Tim shrilled.

Billy, with a late start, rose with them, but the sun blinded him. He saw only Suzy and King leaning, their arms reaching. He saw Suzy's hands opening, saw something white flash between them— something that smashed Billy squarely in the mouth.

Billy opened his eyes in a room without windows. He had not passed out, but the pain was so bad that he had covered his face. He had not wanted anyone to see him crying.

"Billy, you okay now?" a voice said. It was Coach Anderson.

"Yessh," Billy said. His lips didn't work right.

He blinked and looked around. There were fluorescent lights overhead. The room was long and yellow, and several other people lay on narrow beds. Some had bags of ice on their foreheads. The guy on the bed next to Billy smelled of vomit. The baseball game continued on the radio.

"You're in the Met Stadium sick bay," a different voice said. It was a woman holding a blood-pressure strap. Billy thought she was a nurse.

He nodded.

The woman smiled briefly. "I'm Doctor Beth Adams, Billy. You're here because you caught a foul ball, so to to speak."

"With your face, she means," Coach Anderson said.

Billy reached up to touch his lips. "Ahh!" He winced. His lips felt as thick as hot dogs.

"I'm sorry to say you did break a couple of front teeth," the doctor said.

"Shid. Whad am I going to tell my old man?" Billy mumbled.

"I'll run interference for you if need be," the coach said.

Billy stared at the wall. "Naw," he replied. "I'll do it."

The doctor and the coach glanced at each other. "Well, we did we recover the ball," Coach Anderson said brightly. He put it in Billy's hand.

Billy's fingers curled around the baseball. It felt good in his hand. He stared at the white ball and attempted a smile, which hurt like hell.

"Can you sit up now?"

Billy nodded. He hoisted himself up and sat there, blinking.

"When you get back home, you'll need to see your local dentist, who will make some recommendations," the doctor said. "And for now your lips are going to bleed some," she added. "I don't think we'll need stitches. Cold packs should do."

Billy kept blinking as he stared about the room.

"Keep him here one more inning," the doctor said to the coach. "I'll check back before you go. He might need some aspirin for the ride home."

"Thanks, Doc," the coach replied.

Off to the side of the basement recovery room Billy and the coach sat in plastic chairs, listening to the radio. It was the bottom of the seventh. Jim Kaat had given up a couple of hits, and it was now the Orioles four, Twins one. After Jim Palmer had singled, Hal Haydel had relieved Kaat. Billy kept the cold pack to his mouth.

"Shorry, Coash," Billy mumbled. His lips remained numb, though there were pinpricks of pain around the edges. "You should be sheeing the game."

"Hey, you're the one who broke your teeth, not me," the coach said.

Billy looked around for a mirror, but there was none.

Soon a security guard approached them. "Billy Baggs?"

Billy looked up.

"You were the kid hit by the foul ball?"

Billy turned to the coach.

"That's right," the coach said.

"Would you follow me, please?" the guard said, and turned away.

The coach shrugged and gestured for Billy to follow. They accompanied the man down a long, concrete corridor. Huge pipes ran beside them. They could hear faint cheering above them. Then they turned a corner into a larger space and a door with a sign that read PLAYERS AND AUTHORIZED PERSONNEL ONLY.

Billy's eyes widened.

So did Coach Anderson's.

"This way," the guard said, leading them through the door.

Inside they passed along lockers and cubicles with the Twins' names stenciled above them.

KILLEBREW

TOVAR

CARDENAS

MITTERWALD

REESE

OLIVA

And there was gear, bats and pine tar rags and tape lying about, and behind everything was the smell of men's sweat. Billy thought of his father, his woody, wool-shirt smell.

At the end of the locker room, alone on the bench, sat a man with his elbows on his knees and his head in his hands. He sat there in only his undershorts. His gear—shoes, pants, cup, cap, glove—lay scattered around him in a wide circle. Behind the man a trainer was putting the finishing touches on a huge white bandage that held an ice bag tight against the man's left shoulder.

"Mr. Kaat?" the guard said.

The man sitting before the trainer lifted his head and turned to the security guard. His reddish hair was sweaty on his forehead, and his squinty blue eyes were tired.

Billy froze.

"This is the kid," the guard said.

Jim Kaat looked squarely at Billy. His gaze dropped to Billy's mouth. "Looks like you and me had a bad day, son." His eyes, narrow and upturned like a cat's, lightened, and part of a smile came around his lips.

Billy nodded. He began to smile in return, until his lips shot arrows of pain.

Jim Kaat saw Billy wince. "My foul ball must have caught you right in the kisser."

Billy nodded again.

"Came out of the sun," Coach Anderson said. "It was a tough one to see."

Kaat shook hands briefly with Coach Anderson. "Where you folks from?"

"Up north. Flint."

"Good fishing up there," Kaat said, nodding, as the trainer kept working on his shoulder. "I get north once or twice in the fall. In the summers, well, there's not a lot of time for me to go fishing."

The coach smiled.

"Anyway," Kaat said. "I just wanted to say hello to the kid."

"I appreciate it," Coach Anderson said. "Billy's a pitcher himself. Left-hander, like you, and he throws real hard. He's gonna be my ace some day."

"That so?" Kaat said. He smiled for real this time. His eyes dropped to Billy's mouth. "You know, son, if you go home looking like that, your folks ain't gonna let you come down to any more Twins games."

Despite the pain Billy managed a smile.

"Here," Kaat said. He picked up his glove, a long, worn, well-oiled left-hander's glove. "I've been breaking in a new one, and after today's outing, I think it's time to make a change. What's your name again, son?"

Billy could only stare at the big glove.

"Billy Baggs," the coach interjected. "That's with two 'g's."

The trainer handed Kaat a pen, and the pitcher scribbled across the back of the glove, then tossed it to Billy. "You take this old glove home and see what luck it'll bring you. And next time you come down here and I'm batting, use the damn thing, all right, kid?"

Billy and the coach returned to the Flint section in time for the ninth inning. Suzy was gone.

"Where'd you get that?" Tiny Tim said immediately, his eyes locking onto Billy's new glove.

"From Jim Kaat himself," Coach Anderson said.

Tiny Tim, speechless, could only bounce up and down; the fans from Flint crowded around Billy to examine the glove.

"Jim Kaat himself! Wow!"

"Let's see it!" Tim said, reaching out.

"You're sheein' it," Billy mumbled, batting away Tim's hands. He wasn't about to let go of the glove, not in those open bleacher seats, with those timbers that went down forever.

"Can I at least touch it?"

Billy begrudgingly held out the glove.

"Far out!" Tim said, stroking the leather.

"Thash enough," Billy mumbled.

"Billy!" Suzy called. She came through the crowd, King Kenwood following. She went quickly to Billy. "Are you all right? How's your face?"

"Issh okay," Billy said. He tried to screw his face into a no-big-deal look. Air on his broken teeth felt like icicles being driven up his nose into his brain.

"It must really hurt," she murmured, reaching out halfway to touch his lips. King rolled his eyes and looked off to the game.

"Ish no' sho bad," Billy said, one eye on King.

"Can I do anything?" she said, adding "Shut up," as Tim began to make a wisecrack.

"Nod really," Billy mumbled. He looked down so she couldn't see the pain in his eyes.

"You'd better sit down," Suzy said, leading Billy back to their original seats. King, odd man out, headed back to his box seat. Fortunately for Billy, the game ended in ten minutes. Final score: Baltimore 4, Twins 1.

As they streamed onto the bus for the ride home, someone said, "Hey, King, what're you doing here?"

Billy, Suzy and the others looked up.

"Thought I'd try out the bus," King said as he came up the steps. His dark eyes searched for Suzy.

"You're slumming, man," Butch said.

King shrugged. "Somebody can have my spot in the Cadillac."

Suzy turned quickly to Billy. "You should ride in the car. It would be less bumpy, and you'd get home a lot sooner."

"I'm allergic to Cadillacssh," Billy replied. He took his regular seat.

"Hey, why not me?" Butch Redbird exclaimed. "I've never ridden in a Cadillac."

"Sure, why not?" King shrugged.

"Maybe your old man will let me drive!" Butch added as he pushed upstream toward the door.

People settled in. After some negotiations, King took the seat just ahead of Suzy. There was whispering between Jennifer and Suzy, then Jennifer and King, but he got no closer. After a couple of attempts at conversation with Suzy, who kept looking back at Billy, King turned to look out the window.

"The Caddy's already gone." Tim laughed. "Looks like you're stuck with us."

King gave Tim a nasty look, and the bus began to rumble toward the freeway. Once the bus was rolling northward, every twenty minutes or so Billy had to spit some blood out his window. The pain kept him upright in his seat as the bus rolled on. One by one, sunburned and exhausted, the other passengers let their eyes slip shut. Before the sun went down most of them were asleep. King, having given up hope of sitting with Suzy, dozed with his head jolting against the window frame. Tiny Tim leaned against Billy's shoulder and twitched and murmured in some kind of dream. Suzy lay with her head on her arm along the seat back, her ponytail swaying, soft and pale, brushing Billy's knees with slow strokes. Billy cradled his new glove, which was warm and fit his hand surprisingly well. He rolled the foul ball in his fingers. He thought about today.

About Met Stadium.

The forest-tall wooden bleachers, the dark shadows below.

The jetliners overhead.

Suzy's tanned arms reaching for the ball he never saw.

The little girl who gave her ball back.

The woman doctor.

The Twins' locker room.

And one fact that he only now remembered: He had not said a word to Jim Kaat. Not one damn word. He muttered to himself, then, steadying Tim, he leaned up and out the window to spit into the hot twilight air. The side of the bus was painted with thin streamers of blood, as if some bird or small mammal had been hit full speed and broadside. As Billy winced and settled back in, Suzy stirred slightly but didn't awaken. They rode along for another full hour.

Billy watched her sleep, wondering what her dreams were like. He imagined them as lighter, brighter, smoother than his. Her dreams would be of sunny, landscaped, freshly mown lawns; his were often of jungles full of unnamed plants and lurking animals. Billy looked at the white baseball in his glove, rolled its perfect, unending seams. There was a dark smear of blood on the ball, but as the bus grew darker, the sphere glowed whiter and whiter. Suzy's arm drooped over the seat; her hand dangled open and empty. Billy looked at her long, white fingers, at her shining nails. He turned away. Outside the bus window were farms he recognized now; they were only twenty miles from Flint. He took a breath. Leaning forward, he ever so carefully eased the baseball into Suzy's hand. Her sleepy fingers closed around its shape. When she held the ball fully, Billy quickly withdrew his hand.

Her eyelids fluttered.

Billy kept holding his breath; he leaned back and pretended to be mostly asleep.

Her eyes opened halfway. She stared at the ball. "You're giving this to me?" she whispered.

He nodded.

"Why?"

He shrugged. "A shouvenir."

King twitched and jerked at the sound of their voices, as if in a bad dream, but he did not wake up.

When the bus pulled back into Flint, sighing to a stop beside the darkened school, the riders groaned at the sudden brightness of the interior lights. "Geez, you look terrible," Tiny Tim said, drawing back from Billy's face.

"You're no prizhe yourself," Billy said. Tim's face was creased with sleep marks.

King stood up, dazed, his neck bent toward his right shoulder. "God, how do you ride in these things?" he said, peering around the bus.

"Two hours every day," Billy wanted to reply,

but his mouth hurt too much. He squinted at the street. Car headlights and taillights blinked on from the lineup of waiting parents and their vehicles. The Kenwoods' Cadillac sat just below Billy's window. Butch Redbird leaned against it, having a smoke like he owned the car. Several cars down was the Baggses' farm pickup.

"Forget any of your stuff," Bib O'Brien called, "and it belongs to me."

The passengers muttered and slowly stumbled, making their way off the bus. Billy followed Suzy.

Just below the steps King and his father waited for Suzy. "Your dad asked us to give you a ride home," King said, reaching for her bag.

Suzy looked at Billy, then to King. "Okay, sure."

"Did you catch a foul ball?" Mark Kenwood asked Suzy pleasantly. He looked at the ball in Suzy's hand.

Suzy paused. "It's the one from Jim Kaat that hit Billy in the mouth. Billy gave it to me."

King's eyes, hooded and unreadable in the street-light, bored into Billy. Mark Kenwood turned, puzzled, to his son.

Tim said, "Didn't you hear? Billy got to talk to Jim Kaat—and Kaat gave him one of his own baseball gloves."

Mark Kenwood looked back to Billy. "Well, isn't that nice," he said. His face turned steely, and then he spun on his heel and walked toward the Cadillac.

Suzy shrugged and smiled. "See you," she mouthed silently to Billy.

Billy nodded. Despite his battered face, nothing could ruin this moment—not the rusty squeak of the pickup door, not the heavy clomping of his father's boots.

The next morning, with two broken front teeth and his father as angry as hell, Billy made sure to get up on time, five thirty, and have the cows ready for milking. As Abner carried the milker kettle into the barn, its short black air hose looped like a noose around his neck, Billy ducked his head down between cows, where he washed udders and teats.

"The firsh two are ready," he called to his father.

"'Firsh?'" Abner said. "Talk right. It can't be all that bad."

"Ish nosh so bad," Billy mumbled. His lips still felt huge and dead, and the slightest air on his broken teeth struck nerves that channeled into his skull. He passed Abner quickly, heading to the next pair of Holsteins. "Hold on. Let me get a look at you."

Billy turned to face his father.

"You look like you took a left hook from Jack Dempsey."

Billy moved quickly on, kept working.

"Your ma says you want to go in to the dentist," Abner said.

"I didn't shay that. The doctor at the shtadium . . ."

"But do you think you need to see the dentist?" Abner interjected.

"I dunno."

Abner plugged in the air hose, then hung the shiny, stainless milker on the surcingle strap beneath the cow. "In the old days, when people got hurt, they just kept working and got through it." He slipped the four teat cups on, then stood up again. "Nowadays, seems like people run off to the doctor at the drop of a hat."

Billy kept silent. Abner moved on to the next cow. "It shouldn't have happened in the first place. Weren't you paying attention to the damn game?"

Billy's mind filled with images of Suzy Langen's neck and shoulders, her pale hair; for an instant the pain went away.

"Shun got in my eyes, I guesh," he mumbled, and turned to his work.

"That's because you didn't wear your cap," Abner retorted. "Farm kid like you ought to know better." His father stood there, leaning on the cow. The milker went *hissa-chucka, hissa-chucka, hissa-chucka.*

Billy stood to face Abner. "You don't have to shpend your damn money on the dentish. I god my own money. From gopher trapping."

Abner bent to adjust one of the teat cups; there was a sharp squawk and hiss. "That' good, 'cause I ain't." He glared at Billy, then knelt and felt the cow's udder; turning off the vacuum, releasing the teat cups with a sharp noise, he swung out the milker and let loose a steaming white cascade into the milk pail. "Maybe it will teach you to be more careful next time you go off to the city."

"There won't be a next time," Billy muttered sarcastically. "Thass whad you want, ishn't it?"

"What was that remark?" Abner said sharply.

"Nothing," Billy said, lugging the steaming pail of milk away to the bulk tank.

"It better have been nothing," Abner called after him.

At breakfast Abner and Mavis got into a big-time argument about Billy's teeth. Billy grabbed his plateful of eggs and bacon and vamoosed to the porch, where he ate, feeding Skinner a bite now and then.

"I'm just saying lots of people got chipped teeth," Abner said.

"They're not chipped, they're broken," Mavis said. "And how can you expect him to pay for them?"

" 'Cause we don't have dental insurance and 'cause it's his own fault anyway. It will teach him a lesson."

"Don't you think," Mavis said, slowing her words, "that Billy has learned plenty of lessons for a fourteen-year-old?"

Abner was silent.

Mavis continued. "Billy starts high school in two weeks, and his front teeth are going to be fixed before then, whether you like it or not. I'll pay for it myself."

"We need your salary for the farm," Abner replied sharply.

"We'll get by," Mavis said, rattling some dishes loudly. "Ninth grade can be a difficult year. How he looks, how he feels about himself is terribly important."

Abner was silent.

"You must remember what it was like starting high school," Mavis said.

"Sure I do," Abner said flatly. "That was the summer I had polio."

There was silence. Billy turned toward the kitchen, held his breath.

"Oh, Abner—I'm sorry," Mavis said quickly.

His father was silent.

"I wasn't thinking," Mavis murmured.

"Me, I started high school with two leg braces and two crutches," Abner said. "Got so far behind, I never caught up, never finished. That's just how things was back then."

"And you want it to be the same now?" Mavis asked, softer still. "Shouldn't things get a little better with each generation?"

There was a long pause; the only sound was Skinner licking Billy's plate.

"Take him to the dentist then," Abner said, "but make sure he quotes you a price beforehand."

"I will," Mavis said quickly. "He can go in with me this morning."

The clink of Abner's fork on his plate resumed. "And tell that jawbone sawbones that if he goes so much as a dollar over his quote, he'll have me to deal with," Abner added.

Dr. Arnold Arnason's office smelled sweet, like chlorine. Somewhere down a dim hallway his high-speed drill whined liked a giant mosquito. Billy's mother, as it turned out, had already made the appointment. All Billy had to do was wait and wrinkle his nose at the smell and hold tightly to his chair.

"You're a new patient, I believe," said the receptionist, an older woman with half glasses and a pointy chin.

"That's right," Mavis replied.

"Just fill this out, then." The receptionist handed Mavis a form; Billy's mother began writing.

"If you want your dental records sent to us, just sign there on the right." The receptionist pointed.

"Dental records?"

"I presume you've been seeing one of the other dentists in town?"

"No," Mavis said as she wrote. "We Baggses have never had to see a dentist. No cavities for any of us. We think it might be the hard water out our way."

"Everybody has his own theory about tooth care," the woman said. "Dr. Arnason will provide you with facts."

Mavis paused, glanced at the woman's orderly hair and desk, then continued writing.

"I see that you have no dental insurance," the woman said, peering at the sheet. "How will you be paying for this today?"

Mavis looked up, then leaned down quite close to the woman. "How we pay for most things—cash."

"Of course," the woman murmured, drawing back.

Dr. Arnason was a red-nosed, slightly sweaty man of about sixty with strong-smelling aftershave lotion and several fresh razor nicks on his neck. But what Billy saw most of was the interior of Dr. Arnason's nose. Dark hairs bristled and tiny veins spread here and there, and a thin, dried booger way in back flapped back and forth with each breath, and set up a tiny nose whistle.

The dentist tugged on Billy's broken teeth.

Billy groaned.

"Good solid roots," the dentist said. Humming, he turned back and hooked a little vacuum-cleaner-like tube over Billy's jaw, which set up a gurgling sound, after which he sprayed a tiny jet of water on Billy's front teeth.

Billy clenched the sides of his chair. He thought he was going to faint. Or throw up.

"Jackets. We'll have to put jackets on these two," the doctor said, turning to Mavis.

"My husband would like to know how much it will cost," she said.

"About eighty dollars each, temporary for now, and permanent ones in a year or so," the doctor said. "The permanent caps will run a little higher."

"All right," Mavis said, and turned away to let the dentist do his work.

And only a few minutes later, with the smell of glue strongly in his nose, his top lip numb from Novocain, and with two sharp upward yanks from Dr. Arnason, Billy was done. The bright light flashed off. "There you go, son."

Billy sat up groggily, then made his way to the waiting room where his mother sat.

Mavis looked up expectantly. "Let's see," she said with a smile.

Billy drew back his lips in a clumsy attempt at a smile. Mavis's smiled faded; her eyes widened.

"Whasha matter?" Billy said quickly, and closed his mouth.

Dr. Arnason appeared at the desk to hand a chart to the receptionist.

"These . . . these jackets!" Mavis said, taking Billy by the jaw and turning him toward the dentist.

"Is something wrong?"

"I thought . . ." She lowered her voice slightly. "I thought they would be white."

"Those are stainless steel jackets, the temporary kind, until the teeth stop growing," Dr. Arnason said, checking his calendar for the rest of the morning. "All dentists use them."

Mavis glared at him, then took out eight twenty-dollar bills and slapped them, one by one, onto the counter. The receptionist flinched slightly each time.

Afterward, on the street, Billy stopped beside the first auto mirror he saw. He leaned close, took a breath and opened his mouth. For a moment he thought the mirror was defective, that it was glass from a carnival fun-house mirror. Covering his front teeth were two large, gleaming, stainless steel caps. He looked like a Walt Disney rabbit. Like a cartoon version of himself.

"The dentist says they're just temporary," Mavis said.

Billy gave her a stricken look.

"Only a year or so," she added.

Billy was silent.

"Do they hurt?"

He shook his head.

"Well, that's good," Mavis said, trying to be upbeat.

They stood there. Billy checked the mirror again.

"I've still got a half hour free," Mavis said as she checked her watch. "Why don't we walk down to the bakery, then go to Krepsbach's and find some school clothes for you?"

"I ain't going to school this year," Billy said.

"Sure you are," Mavis said easily.

Billy trudged after his mother. Walking down Main Street in the morning sunlight, he kept leaning close to the store and café windows they passed and baring his teeth. He didn't notice the people who stared out strangely at his grimaces. All Billy saw, reflected in the glass, was the gleam of stainless steel.

They lingered at the bakery over Bismarcks. Billy kept wiping his numb lips and cheeks to make sure he wasn't slobbering or wearing a mustache of red jelly. "You look fine," Mavis said.

"Right," Billy muttered. He felt little pinpricks in his lips. Some of the feeling was returning.

"Remember, they are temporary," Mavis said.

Billy let out an exasperated breath.

"School clothes," she said brightly. "Let's talk about school clothes."

"I ain't going to school looking like this," Billy said again.

"You look fine," Mavis replied.

At Krepsbach's Department Store, Billy followed his mother along the aisles as she plucked up underwear, T-shirts and socks, then headed toward blue jeans and flannel shirts. Her idea of a successful shopping trip, whether to the grocery store or clothing store, was to never come to a complete stop. Billy gave up following her and waited beside a rack of dress slacks; he touched their fabric, a shiny hard rayon blend, with fashionably narrow legs. Close by were bright madras-patterned shirts. He wondered where King Kenwood bought his clothes.

"What do you see there?" Mavis asked, arriving with a pair of jeans in hand, circling the rack.

"Nothing," Billy said. He glanced across to the cheaper section where they had always shopped, then back to the fashionable area.

"You'll need a good pair of slacks this year," his mother said.

"No I won't," Billy said. "I was just looking."

"That's what shopping is, looking," Mavis said

as her hand fanned the row of slacks. She removed a pair of light-brown, sharply creased slacks and found a checkered madras shirt to go with them. "Come. I want you to try these on."

"But these are expensive. What about Pa?"

"You only start ninth grade once. And anyway, I've got my own money," his mother replied.

Billy sighed and followed her toward the little changing room. Soon, wearing all new clothes, he stepped out and looked in the mirror.

"Wow!" his mother said. Billy blinked. His mouth came open nearly to a smile—until he remembered his steel teeth.

They left Krepsbach's with two large bags and a shoe box. Inside the shoe box was a pair of fine brown leather penny loafers. "On the first day of high school you're going to look like a million bucks," Mavis said.

"I'm gonna look like Bugs Bunny," Billy said.

"In just a few days people won't give your teeth another look," his mother said.

"I will," he said.

He and Mavis parted at the Doctors' Clinic steps, where, as agreed, Mavis handed him the keys to the pickup. "You drive straight home, now," she said sternly.

"Sure, Ma," Billy said. Like most farm kids, he got to drive sooner than most young people. He was only a few months away from getting his farm permit, which would allow him, at age fifteen, to drive legally to town on farm business. At present he got by because he was a tall farm kid in a small farming town.

"Straight home," she said, raising one eyebrow.

"I have to make some turns," Billy said. There was nothing like car keys in hand to bring back his naturally sunny sense of humor.

"You know what I mean," she replied. "I'll get a lift home tonight with Mrs. Pederson."

He started up the engine and, sitting squarely in the seat, drove carefully off; he knew Mavis was watching him from the clinic steps. When his mother was out of sight, he accelerated sharply, flopped one elbow out the window and turned toward Green Lawn, where Suzy Langen lived.

Green Lawn, a development of handsome ranch homes, was Flint's upper-class suburb. Doctors, dentists, lawyers and judges lived here. At curbside each home sported a mailbox designed to resemble a loon, or a Siamese cat, or an eagle. One had an ancient, white-painted single-bottom plow sitting on a bed of crushed red rock; atop its curving iron perched a miniature red barn mailbox. Scrap-iron art. Billy spat out his window. The only thing these Green Lawn mailboxes lacked in the way of country realism was a bullet hole or two.

He drove on, slowly. The Baggses' farm pickup looked like a turd in a punch bowl as it drifted past the landscaped lawns of Venus Lane. But there was no law against driving by. Kneeling close by the sidewalk was a woman working among bright-red geraniums. She gave him a long stare. In reply Billy bared his metal teeth and made a face. Her eyes widened, and she clutched her trowel.

Soon, up ahead and on the right, Billy saw it: 1869 Venus Lane. It was a long, low white-brick ranch with green globes of shrubbery out front. Through the wide picture window he saw a sunburst clock. Long, pale couches. A tall china cabinet. He slowed further. Stared. Then, in the worst timing possible, the front door opened and Suzy Langen, dressed in shorty pajamas, dashed out to the mailbox. Billy froze at the wheel; the pickup lurched to a stop directly in front of Suzy.

She squinted uncertainly at the old truck. Then her eyes widened. "Billy!"

Billy's lower jaw moved a couple of times, but he could pump out no words.

Her long arms remained stretched out toward the mailbox, her hands held a thick letter, and the sunlight shone within her pajama top. The curves there took Billy's breath away.

"Billy, what are you doing? Why are you here?" Her face flushed, and she looked again at the letter in her hand, then quickly put it in the mailbox and clamped the door shut. She crossed her arms over her chest.

"Me?" Billy said stupidly. "I was just . . . driving by."

"You don't have a license."

"I've got my farm permit. Almost."

Her gaze dropped to his arms, to his hands on the steering wheel. Then she stepped closer. "How's your mouth? You were in to see the doctor this morning, weren't you?"

"Dentist," Billy said.

"Are you okay?" She leaned toward his window; in her hair he could smell her bed, her pillow. "Let me see them."

"Naw, they're fine," Billy managed to reply.

"Show me." She sounded like the doctor, the woman doctor at the stadium. For an instant he saw Suzy as an adult, dressed in white and wearing a stethoscope. He turned to face her and opened his lips.

For a long moment she was silent. Somewhere on a lawn a robin chirped. "Well . . . you look a lot better than you did last night," she offered.

"I do?" Billy mumbled.

"Sure." She smiled, stepped back slightly and glanced toward the mailbox. "It's crazy that I'd see you right now. I was just writing my pen pal about the trip yesterday."

Billy nodded.

"I told her everything, I mean, the trip and all, but also how I got the foul ball, that it had blood-stains on it and everything." She blushed slightly.

Billy stared. "Suzy, would you like to do some-thing sometime? I mean, together?"

Suzy paused. She glanced behind her, at her house and the neighborhood. Then she turned back to him. "As in a date?"

He nodded.

"Maybe," she answered. "What would we do?" A small smile lifted the corners of her lips.

Do. That he had not considered. "Go for a ride?"

"Possibly. When?"

"Like . . . now."

"I can't go now!"

"Why not?" Billy said.

There was silence, long moments of it. Billy swung open the passenger door; in a flash Suzy hopped inside. He didn't think about the worn seat that smelled of barn, or the broken fan belt on the dashboard, or the battered bolts that littered the floor. He hit the gas pedal and yanked his foot from the clutch, and with a sharp chirp of tire rubber they were off. Driving he knew.

"So where you want to go?" Billy asked, leaning back, steering with one hand.

"Just around the block," she said quickly. She kept both hands on the dashboard.

"Around the block? That's not very far."

"Where then?"

"How about down Main Street?"

"We can't drive down Main Street!" she gasped.

"Why not?"

"What if someone saw me?"

"They won't," Billy said.

With Suzy slouched very low in the seat Billy drove down Main Street. People crossed here and there; Billy slowed to let them pass. Then Coach Anderson himself came out of the bakery carrying a loaf of bread; he spotted Billy and hailed him. "Damn," Billy said. He had no choice but to stop.

"Oh, shit!" Suzy whispered.

"Stay low," Billy hissed.

She dropped to the floor and wedged herself between the gearshift and his legs.

"Hello, Billy," the coach called. "How'd it go at the dentist this morning?"

"Fine. Sort of." Billy tried to fill his window with his head and shoulders so the coach couldn't see inside. He opened his lips.

"I see what you mean," the coach said, examining Billy's new teeth. He smiled. "Let's just say that they give you character."

"I had enough character already," Billy replied.

The coach chuckled; below, Suzy clung tighter to his legs.

"Well, car behind," Billy said, glancing into the mirror. "Got places to go."

"Farm business, right?" the coach said, winking as he glanced at the truck.

"Absolutely, Coach," Billy said, holding up the broken fan belt from the dash.

"You've been carrying that old belt around all summer."

"My ma's idea," Billy said. "Cop stops me, I just tell him I'm headed to the parts store."

"Smart woman, your mother." The coach chuckled. Billy waved and drove on.

Suzy let out a long breath. "What if he'd seen me?"

"But he didn't, did he?"

Suzy peeked over the dashboard. "You'd better take me home."

"Why so soon?"

"Because. That's why." She was angry.

Billy turned dutifully toward Green Lawn. As he drove, carefully and obediently, Suzy slowly rose up higher in the seat. As they passed through the tidy, winding streets, Billy said, "So where does King live?"

She looked at him. "Why?"

Billy shrugged. "Just curious."

"There," she said, and pointed. Billy looked left, across to a long, expensive-looking brick house with a three-car garage and a lawn that looked like a golf course. Some sort of netting or cage was partially visible behind the house.

"Must be nice," he said.

She was silent.

Billy slowed for a closer look. She shrank lower in the seat.

"Afraid King will see us?" Billy asked, glancing her way.

"He's out jogging. And anyway, I don't want anyone to see us," she said.

"But what if he saw us together?"

"So what?" Suzy said.

"He'd be pissed, that's what," Billy answered.

"It's not like he's my boyfriend."

"So what is he then?"

Suzy sat up after they had passed the Kenwoods' house. "King and I grew up together. Same street. Same neighborhood. Same baby-sitter. Our parents went on all their vacations together. We were always together as kids; his mother has all these old home movies of us. We spent so much time together that King's just protective of me, I guess."

"To say the least," Billy said.

"You don't know him; he's very complex," Suzy said, annoyance in her voice.

"I know him well enough," Billy said. "He's a jerk."

"Well, he thinks you're one, too," she replied, and folded her arms across her chest.

They drove along in silence.

"The thing is, you two just don't know each other," Suzy said. "For example, King's very smart. He always gets the highest scores in our whole grade on the Iowa Basic tests, but few people know that. Also, his mother drinks way too much. Plus he's obsessed with playing professional baseball, like his brother."

"Poor little King," Billy remarked.

Suzy let out an exasperated breath. "I just wish you and King could get along."

"I can't see how," Billy said.

"What is it between you two?" she asked. "Is it the pitching? The baseball stuff?"

"More than that," Billy said. They passed the golf course that ran along the back side of Green Lawn. The green fairways were like perfect fields. "There's some bad blood between our families."

"From this summer? When your father went to jail?"

Billy nodded.

"Then Abner must hate my father, too," Suzy said.

"True, but it's more than that." His eyes strayed over her body.

"I knew it," she said. "It's me."

He smiled and shook his head sideways. "More even than you. I think King and I were born to get under each other's skin."

"I don't believe it has to be that way," Suzy said.

"I do," Billy said.

They drove along the clean streets of Green Lawn in silence.

"Let me out by that birdhouse mailbox," Suzy said. "I'll cut through the backyard."

Billy reluctantly obeyed. When the truck was stopped, he paused. "So . . . what about you and me?" he asked.

"What about it?" She got out and stood there in the sunlight.

He swallowed. "Can I see you again?"

"Maybe." She folded her arms across her chest and moved a pebble with a bare toe.

"Why only maybe?"

"Because." She put her hands on her hips. "Because you have too much anger, and you do stupid things just to show off. Also, you downright scare me sometimes."

He set his jaw and looked away. "I don't mean to do that."

"I know," she said. Her voice softened. "And I really hate to say it, but that's what I like about you."

He turned to her.

"Plus it's fun being scared once in a while," she

said. She leaned over and gave him a quick kiss on his sore cheek, and was gone.

On the way out of Green Lawn, who should Billy see but King Kenwood. He was jogging toward home wearing sweats and ankle weights; his shirt was darkly wet down the front. King wiped his eyes and squinted more closely at the truck.

Billy slowed and put his head out the window. "Hey there, Archer, need a lift?"

King did a double-take at Billy behind the wheel. He drew up. "No. I'm . . . in training."

"Suit yourself," Billy said, and drove on. In his rearview mirror he saw King look suddenly toward Suzy's house, then again to the Baggses' pickup.

Driving the back roads, Billy sped toward home. The tires rattled over washboarded gravel, but he floated on cloud nine. Make that cloud ten. He touched his cheek. It was warm where Suzy had kissed him. Smiling as he thought of the morning sunlight blooming in Suzy's pajama top, and of her long fingers on the dashboard, he cruised straight down the center of the road.

Soon he was home. Ahead was the tall row of poplars that Abner had planted to shield the farm from the view of passersby. Just inside their leafy wall was the narrow white house, the low barn and outbuildings in need of paint, the cow-lot fence in need of new posts, the empty ball field and the old farm implements scattered here and there. At center yard his father hunched over a bright spark of the welder as he worked on the manure spreader. Billy drove right up to him.

Abner, wearing a welder's hood, turned and

raised the gray mask. His dark hair was sweaty on his forehead.

"Hi, Pa."

Abner set down the torch, turned off the power. "So. Let's see what I got for my money," he said. He stepped closer to squint at Billy's teeth.

Billy opened his mouth.

"Jesus," Abner said. He spit tobacco juice to the side. "Come hunting season you're going to have to keep your mouth closed."

"Why so, Pa?"

"The glare from those teeth would frighten a deer into the next county."

Billy nodded agreeably. "You're probably right, Pa."

Abner's eyes ran up and down Billy.

"Anything you need help with?" Billy asked.

Abner removed his mask all the way. "That dentist give you too much laughing gas?"

Billy chuckled. "Naw, I'm just in a good mood."

Abner was silent. He scratched his long chin. "Well, if you're in such a good mood, then get your working clothes on. The gutter needs cleaning."

"No problem, Pa," Billy said, and headed into the house.

Abner watched him, scratching his head as Billy crossed the yard, trying to whistle through his new front teeth even though they still hurt.

Later that day, after Mavis was home, Abner spotted the bags of new school clothes.

"Good God!" he said. "Who do you think I

am, King Midas?"

"It's not all your money," Mavis said sharply.

Abner blinked.

"When Billy starts high school, he's going to make a good first impression," Mavis said.

"Who on?"

"The teachers. The principal. The other kids who don't know Billy," Mavis answered.

"High school is high school; it's not some kind of social affair."

"High school is a lot of things all wrapped into one," Mavis said.

"I wouldn't know," Abner said.

"You want to at least look at Billy's new clothes?" She began to open the sacks.

Abner rattled open the local newspaper. "I'll see them when school starts."

Mavis turned to Billy. Nothing and no one could dampen his mood. He took the bags up to his room and tried on his new clothes. His new loafers squeaking when he moved, Billy stood stiffly back from his small round mirror. He could see only parts of himself at once. The clothes parts looked fine. The head part looked like a yellow-haired kid with squinty eyes and stainless steel teeth. He adjusted the mirror again to see his shoes and narrow-legged pants. He practiced standing with his hands in his pockets. He practiced holding imaginary books. He imagined himself in high school, in the crowded hallway. He pretended to look up with surprise. "Why hello, Suzy," he said.

He cleared his throat, tried a deeper pitch. "Good afternoon, Suzy."

As he tried yet another voice, he heard the floorboards of the hallway squeak. Turning quickly, he saw his mother, come to check on his clothes. She was standing at his door.

"How about, 'Hello, King'?" Mavis offered. "Maybe that's who you should be trying to get acquainted with. A little courtesy goes a long way."

Billy, annoyed, stepped away from the mirror. "He doesn't talk to me; why should I talk to him?"

"You two might find out you have some things in common."

"I doubt it," Billy said.

Mavis sat on the edge of his bed. "By the way, what were you doing driving in Green Lawn today?"

Billy pretended to check the length of a cuff. "Green Lawn?"

"Green Lawn."

Billy cleared his throat. He tried to buy time. "Who said I was driving around Green Lawn?"

"It doesn't matter who. I just want to know why. After all, you promised me you would drive straight home."

Billy shrugged. "I . . . just made a few turns, that's all."

"Past Suzy Langen's house?" Mavis said.

Billy set his jaw. He would not look at his mother.

"Billy, I don't want to meddle in your life," she began, "but Suzy Langen—"

"Then don't!" he said.

She bit her lower lip. Appeared to count to ten. "All right, I won't," she said.

She got up. At the doorway she turned. "But you're done driving unless your pa or I am with you. That's your punishment for lying."

8

Billy was so mad at his mother that he did not speak to her for two days—days when there was no chance to go to town, no chance to see Suzy, no chance to do anything. The August weather continued hot and windy, and the silage corn was drying on its stalks. Since the ground was hard enough to support the big tractor, the corn chopper and wagons, this meant it was silo-filling time. He swore his parents had arranged for this weather.

Monday afternoon, weighted by tools, Billy climbed the outside ladder of the silo. The ladder was hip narrow, with thirty iron rungs; there was no safety cage. Fastened on his belt was a fist-sized pulley, and around his waist, one end of a wrist-thick rope. Near the top the breeze was cooler inside his shirt. He held tighter to the iron. Finally he pulled himself into the little iron crow's nest and took a look across the farm. He spit, something Robert had always done, down the forty feet to the ground. He watched the wispy, pale streamer swirl through air currents, watched it shrink until it disappeared. Robert was right: You could never see it hit the ground.

"Let's go," Abner called impatiently from below.

Right in the middle of raising the blower pipe, and a sure bet to irritate Abner, a car pulled into the yard. It was the Goldberg family's late-model station wagon, and Aaron Goldberg hopped out and waved to Billy. The Goldbergs, from Minneapolis, were staying at a lake near Flint for the whole summer. Overprotective parents, they were trying to keep Aaron safe from peace protests and "bad influences" in the city. Aaron had shown up for the first Friday-night baseball game and become a regular visitor on the farm from that day on. He was a kid who, like Tiny Tim in town, had attached himself to Billy. "What can I do to help?" Aaron shouted up to Billy as his parents drove off.

"Climb up onto the bottom rung and hold the lower end of the blower pipe so it doesn't scrape against the concrete," Billy called, and pointed. Goldberg was actually useful at times.

Aaron scrambled up and steadied the pipe, and Billy gave Abner the go-ahead signal once again.

Soon the three of them had the pipe positioned vertically against the side of the silo. At the top Billy turned the curved hood until it pointed dead center inside the silo, then secured it with heavy wire. Climbing halfway down the silo, he tightened another wire, then finally dropped from the last rung down to the ground. He turned to face Goldberg. Aaron was a head shorter than Billy, and his bushy hair made him look as skinny as a cornstalk. Billy gave him a Cheshire grin. Aaron did a double take at the sight of Billy's new teeth.

"What the heck happened to you?"

"It's a long story," Billy said, pretending to yawn.

"Well, geez, let's hear it."

Billy stepped off to the side and retrieved his Jim Kaat glove from the pickup. He tossed it to Goldberg. Aaron's jaw dropped as he read the autograph. Cradling the glove like it was a newborn baby, he breathed, "If you don't tell me the story, I'm gonna have a cardiac."

Billy gave him the short version, which left Aaron taking deep breaths. "Jim Kaat himself—oh man, oh man."

Abner drove up on the tractor.

"Unbelievable, Mr. Baggs! A real glove from Jim Kaat!"

Abner stared down at the glove, then at Billy's teeth. "Son, sometimes it's hard to tell good luck from bad," he said dryly.

Billy gave him a cross look.

"Oh no; this is definitely a good sign, Mr. Baggs," Aaron said, stroking the glove, examining its signature once again. Earlier in the summer, when Abner had returned home from his stay in jail, he was about as friendly as an old bear just out of his den, and Billy had worried about having anyone, especially a city kid like Aaron Goldberg, hanging around the farm. But Aaron loved to work, whether pitching bales, shoveling oats or fixing fences, and since he was also careful around machinery, Abner had no complaints about Aaron Goldberg. Also, a third person—a kind of buffer between Billy and Abner—was good to have right now. So far Abner had said nothing about Suzy Langen, but it was just a matter of time.

"I'll need the full story," Aaron said, handing the glove back to Billy, "but first things first. When do we start filling the silo, Mr. Baggs?"

Abner's brown eyes gleamed with a trace of humor. He squinted across to the field, then briefly up at the sun. "Tomorrow," he said, "first thing after morning chores."

"What's my job going to be?"

"I'll find something, don't you worry about that."

"We'll need to be done by Friday night," Aaron said.

"And why is that?" Abner said, squinting down at Aaron. His narrow face held a trace of a smile.

"It's the last Farm Team game of the summer, Mr. Baggs."

"It had better be," Abner said, his smile receding. He glanced once at Billy, then across and over to the homemade baseball field beyond the barn. "I've had my fill of strangers invading the farm every Friday night."

"It hasn't been every Friday night," Aaron interjected.

Abner shot Aaron a glare, then continued. "It takes a whole day Saturday to clean up after people, plus I need my corncrib put back to being a corncrib rather than a damn concession stand."

"We'll get it changed back," Billy said.

"It ain't like we needed extra work around here," Abner groused.

"You're absolutely right," Aaron said, "so I was thinking that for the last game of the summer, we ought to ask people to make a small donation, say when they park, to cover some of the expenses."

"You're a kid after my own heart," Abner said. He glanced at the sky. "But we've got to finish silo filling before there's any more baseball on this farm."

"No sweat," Billy said.

"We'll see," Abner replied, and limped off.

Aaron watched him go. "Secretly, your father likes the ball games."

"I doubt that," Billy said.

"I know he does. Want to know why?"

Billy turned to Aaron.

"Because it gives him an opportunity to talk about you to strangers."

He stared at Aaron.

"It's true. You should hear him brag."

Billy looked across the yard to his father, at work now on a silage wagon.

"He says that you're going to make it to the major leagues someday."

Billy spit. "Fat chance," he said, and headed across toward the silo.

"If you do, can I be your agent?" Aaron said, trotting alongside.

"Sure," Billy answered, his eyes traveling to the tall, empty silo, "on one condition."

"What's that?"

"You tramp silage all week."

"Deal," Aaron said.

Billy laughed loudly for the first time in days.

"What? What?" Aaron said quickly.

"Tramping silage is only the worst job on the farm."

"So?" Aaron said. "A sports agent has to start somewhere."

Aaron continued to rattle on as they greased the silage blower, but Billy was all business. He wanted no problems between now and Friday night, his chance to see Suzy and to show King Kenwood a real fastball.

The dry weather held, and silo filling proceeded. Aaron tramped raw silage beneath the blower pipe. This meant walking around and around inside the silo, leveling, stomping, packing the chopped corn that came roaring down, green and damp and pelting, from the curved hood of the pipe. The other tramper was Big Danny Boyer, a giant silent kid (actually in his twenties) from down the road. Billy tried to imagine King Kenwood, dressed in coveralls, doing this work, but he couldn't. The human imagination had its limits.

"Friday-night ball for sure!" Aaron called through green rain.

Silo filling continued. Like most major operations on the farm, there were hazards. Each day before the trampers entered the silo, Abner made sure to run the silage blower, empty, for several minutes. Its great fan flushed away any trace of silo gas, a kind of methane generated from fermenting corn that every summer killed several farmers in the Midwest. By Thursday, without injury or mechanical breakdown of any kind, they had made great progress. The cornfield was three-quarters stubble, Aaron was as green-colored and strong-smelling as an Irish leprechaun dipped in corn whiskey, and the two trampers were within a long fork's reach of the silo's rim.

"Baseball tomorrow night, Mr. Baggs!" Aaron said.

"We'll see," Abner said. He was clearly pleased.

If the flow of wagons and outside work was seamless and steady, noon dinner was another matter. Silo filling required many hands, and Mavis, her first summer working in town, had hired two neighbor girls, Heather and Gina Erickson, to help out with cooking for the men. The girls were stubby redheads. Heather was barely sixteen; Gina was thirteen but looked eighteen, at least on top. Both girls had short legs, short vocabularies and even shorter tempers. Heather's baby, Dale, slept blissfully on the couch.

"Shit; we're behind. You were supposed to set the table already," barked the older sister.

"I set it yesterday."

"No you dint. And look—the gravy is burning."

"It ain't either; it's supposed to be brown."

"Stir the damn gravy or I'll whip your ass with a wooden spoon. And where's the bread?"

"Kiss my brown star," Gina replied.

"Girls, girls—none of that language!" Abner

boomed. He, Billy, Aaron and Big Danny sat at the table, hopeful of food sometime in the near future. "The bread is in the bread drawer," he said, pointing.

"See, shithead, I told you there was bread," Heather said to Gina. Compared to Suzy Langen, as tall and graceful as a show cat, the Erickson girls were scrappy barn cats. Billy couldn't imagine how he had once found Heather—even, very recently, Gina—worth lusting after.

But Aaron Goldberg watched Gina move back and forth like the kitchen was a tennis court and she was a bouncing ball. Because of the heat in the kitchen, both girls wore short shorts and bathing suit tops. Gina leaned against Aaron—on purpose, it was clear to Billy—as she arranged his silverware just so. Aaron's face flushed. Billy winked at Aaron across the table and began to fan himself.

Aaron didn't notice. His eyes were welded to Gina like it was a hot Fourth of July and she was a double-scoop ice-cream cone. Gina gave Billy a smug look. One of her shoulder straps had slipped, and she didn't bother to fix it. Actually, Gina had her moments, Billy was forced to admit. Big Danny sat there, straight-backed in his chair, and stared eagerly at both girls.

"Lord let us pray," Heather said, "that this food don't kill anyone."

And, with such a blessing, noon dinner was served.

"Well," Abner said to Aaron, as he passed the

potatoes, "who are you boys playing Friday night—assuming the silo is full by then?"

"It'll be full," Billy said.

"Town Team, a rematch," Aaron answered.

"And it's not just boys," Gina yelled from the kitchen. "Heather and I are on Farm Team, too."

"Speaking of boys, will King Kenwood be there?" Heather asked. "He's got the grooviest eyes."

"As if he'd look at you!" Gina said.

"Shut up!" Heather barked.

"A rematch." Abner nodded. "I guess they didn't like getting whipped last time."

"They're gonna appreciate it even less this time," Billy said.

"Who'll be pitching for the town boys?" Abner asked.

"I hope it's King," Heather said.

"Me, too," Abner said. "He strikes me as a kid who every once in a while needs to be taken down a notch."

"Or two," Billy added.

By noon on Friday, silage began to spray out the top of the silo like green confetti falling onto a parade. Aaron appeared in the doorway and waved his white T-shirt from a pitchfork. In the roar of the blower, Abner drew a hand across his throat, and Billy cut the power. "Wahoo! Baseball tonight!" Aaron yelled from high above.

After serving a final lunch of of meat loaf, crumbling cake and watery red Jell-O, the Erickson girls left. It was Billy's job to drive Big Danny home.

"Come straight back!" Abner said, "and don't tell your ma."

Billy headed off with Aaron and Big Danny in the pickup. He made up several minutes' time by driving seventy miles an hour to Danny's place—Aaron clutching the dashboard all the way—then roared back to Riverbend. The Ericksons' Ford was there, as he knew it would be.

"Here's the plan," Billy said, making sure not to slam the truck door. Aaron squinted ahead, through the trees, to where there was the sound of laughing and splashing.

"I'm not sure we have time for this," Aaron said. "Remember, we've got a game tonight."

"You're just chicken," Billy whispered.

Aaron swallowed nervously.

They sneaked along the trail, then peeped out through the leaves. On the big rocks of Riverbend, Heather sat with her back to them, nursing her baby. In the water Gina floated on her stomach, as plump and naked as a peach.

"She's got built-in life preservers," Billy observed.

"No kidding!" Aaron breathed.

"Come on out, wherever you are," Gina called in a singsong voice. She didn't bother to look their way. "We know it's you—Billy and Aaron, Billy and Aaron."

"So what if it wasn't us?" Billy said as they emerged from the bushes. He turned sideways as he shed his itchy, corn-smelling clothes.

"Gina? She wouldn't care." Heather sniffed.

Gina just laughed and submerged in the blue water.

Billy dove in, gasping at the cold water on his private parts; surfacing, he spit and cleared his eyes. "Well?" he called to Aaron.

"Well what?" Aaron said.

"You comin' in?"

"Sure," Aaron muttered. He stepped behind some rocks. Then he slipped, white and squirrel skinny, into the water.

Billy let the water flow over him. It was like cold velvet. Summers he carried a bar of Ivory soap in the truck, and now he sudsed himself top to bottom.

"I could use some of that," Aaron said, coming closer to where Billy and Gina swam.

"Want me to help scrub?" Gina teased.

"No—I can do it!" Aaron said quickly, trying to swim and hold on to the slippery white soap at the same time. They laughed as he sank and coughed up water.

In a minute or two Aaron was clean. The three of them dog-paddled and spit water, then hung on the rocks and let the water turn their bodies downstream. "Why don't you come in, Heather?" Billy called.

She looked backward over her shoulder, held up the baby and shrugged.

"Sorry," Billy said. "I forgot."

"Me too, sometimes," she said wistfully.

"Lay him on the riverbank," Gina said. "He ain't going anywhere."

"Some mother you'd make," Heather said.

"Well, I ain't gonna be one soon," Gina said.

"Keep showing off your titties and you will be," Heather replied.

"Knock it off, you two," Billy said to the sisters.

Gina paddled closer to Aaron, then suddenly rose partway onto a flat, warm boulder beside him. "So what's the plan for tonight's game with the Town Team?"

"Plan?" Aaron replied. His mouth dropped open as he stared at plump, slick Gina. Even Billy let out a breath. She had definitely grown up.

"Last time when you were coach you had me batting last." She pouted.

"He's still the coach," Billy said.

"Plus now I'm your agent, too," Aaron added. He did not take his eyes from Gina.

"True," Billy said, grinning.

"Anyway I hate being last at anything," Gina said, "so I want to bat higher in the order."

"Keep her last," Heather called.

"Like where?" Aaron managed to ask Gina, blinking river water from his eyes.

"Like lead off."

"Lead off? Okay," Aaron said in a faraway voice.

From above them on the rocks, Heather laughed sarcastically.

"You'll see," Gina said instantly, splashing water at them and at her sister, too.

On the drive home, Aaron looked back at the woods and trees of Riverbend. "You know what, Billy? I can't wait to get back to school."

"Are you nuts?"

"In English class, Mrs. Lancombe will give us the standard essay assignment: 'What I did last summer.'"

Billy sped along. "So what are you going to write?"

"How I saw my first naked girl," Aaron said. He leaned back in the seat, his hand trailing out the window, totally relaxed as Billy sped onward.

Billy parked near the barn and hustled Aaron inside before Abner could see their wet hair. "Here," he said, handing Aaron a manure fork. "I never did clean the gutter today, plus we've got the milking to do."

"No problem," Aaron murmured, and contentedly set to work shoveling cowshit. Billy checked the clock. "I'll be right back," he said.

In the quiet, empty house he took a deep breath and dialed Suzy's number. He waited, thinking of clever phrases, but he froze when Mrs. Langen answered.

"Hello? Hello?"

"Is . . . Suzy there?" he managed to say.

"No, she isn't."

"Oh. This is . . . King."

"King? You don't sound like yourself."

"Summer cold or something." He faked a cough.

85

"Well, dear, I hope it won't affect your game tonight," she said.

"So she knows about the game?"

"Well, sure. You called earlier and told her. Didn't you?"

"Oh, that's right," Billy said. He managed another cough. "Must be this cold medicine."

She laughed. "Well get better, King dear. We don't want to get beaten again by those nasty farm kids, do we?"

Billy coughed, for real this time.

By five P.M. their neighbor, Ole Svendson, had taken up his post as parking attendant. Ole was a narrow-shouldered bachelor who kept to himself. On Friday nights he organized spectator parking at the Baggs farm like a Border collie fretting over sheep. "People think they can park any damn place they please!" Ole called across the yard.

Billy and Aaron waved politely from the barn door.

"It wouldn't hurt to straighten out that tractor and those bicycles, either," Ole added, pointing across the yard with his cattle cane.

"Maybe in a previous life he was a Chicago traffic cop," Aaron said.

By six o'clock they had finished the milking and rushed into the house to shower and change. Billy put on a fresh white T-shirt over his best black jeans, and then they hastily ate bologna sandwiches for supper. Mavis was working late, which was fine by Billy; that way she couldn't spy on him.

Before heading outside, Billy slipped into the bathroom for one last look in the mirror. In the medicine cabinet, behind several old pill bottles, was a glass bottle of Mennen aftershave. It had been a gift from Mavis to Abner, when times were good, when Robert was alive. The bottle was dusty and only a quarter empty. Billy uncapped the container. Suddenly all four of them were squeezed into the pickup heading into town on a Saturday night for ice cream and roller skating. Abner had worn aftershave, his mother light perfume; Billy had not smelled either since.

Billy closed his eyes as he inhaled the scent. When he opened them, he stared at the little green flask, then began to tuck it back into its hiding place—but in mid motion he changed his mind. He splashed some onto his hands, then patted his neck and, for good measure, his armpits. He sneezed once from the minty vapor, then stashed the bottle and attended to his hair. Slicking the yellow thatch as best he could beneath his cleanest cap, a freebie from last spring's John Deere Daze, he straightened to smile into the mirror. His stainless teeth gleamed; his smiled collapsed. He tried smiling without showing his teeth this time. "Why hello, Suzy," he mumbled to the mirror.

"Well hello yourself, big guy," warbled Aaron Goldberg, who had come in to check his own hair.

"You've had it now!" Billy chased Aaron into the yard.

Not long after six, more of the Farm Team began to arrive.

The shaggy-haired McGinty brothers, Bob and Owen, whose family ran a sheep farm in the rocky north end of Flint County.

Gina, Heather and baby Dale, whom somebody on the bench would have to hold when Heather batted. Billy hoped it wasn't him; little Dale had a habit of getting excited by the cheering and filling his pants.

Big Danny Boyer, who went immediately to right field, where he stood like a lone oak tree.

Shawn Howenstein, the butcher's son, who always smelled of tallow and had red bits of hamburger under his fingernails; Skinner made a beeline for Shawn and licked at his arms.

And, to Billy and Aaron's great relief, the battered station wagon with a rack of shining, short-handled hoes atop: the González family. They were migrant workers who lived near Monterrey, Mexico. Every summer they came north to work in the sugar-beet fields seventy or so miles west of Flint, in the Red River Valley near the Minnesota–North Dakota border. Passing through Flint, they had seen the flier for Farm Team baseball, and now were regulars on Friday evenings. Without Raúl González at second and Jesús at short, the Farm Team's infield was as full of holes as a prairie dog town.

"*Buenos días,*" Billy called as the stern-faced Mr. González drove the wagon past Ole Svendson into the front yard. Manuel González nodded ever so slightly.

"Hey—you can't park there!" Ole called. He waved his cane.

"Players' entrance; it's all right," Aaron replied quickly. "But thank you, Mr. Svendson. You're doing a fine job."

Ole muttered something and turned back to man the gates.

Billy saw Mrs. González, framed in the open window of the old wagon. "*Hola*, Billy," she said. María González was a tired-looking woman with a couple of missing teeth. Her round face, though weathered by fieldwork, retained a dark beauty; her eyes were as shiny as black walnuts.

Billy nodded and smiled to her.

Raúl and Jesús emerged, slim and smooth as deer. Raúl was eleven, and Jesús was Billy's age. Both wore old, thin, homemade baseball gloves that seemed grown to their hands like extra layers of skin or callus.

"*Que pasa?*" Billy asked. He had learned a few Spanish words and phrases this summer, mainly by listening hard, then repeating them later, when he was alone.

"*Nada,*" Raúl said, grinning shyly.

"The same old shit," Jesús added.

"Jesús!" his mother barked, glaring at her oldest son.

But by then the two González brothers were trotting toward the field, flipping a baseball expertly between them. Their sister, Gloria, remained in the car holding the sleeping toddler, Juan Elvis.

"Your mother is home, Billy?" María González asked, looking expectantly toward the house. She and Mavis had quickly become friends.

"She'll be home from work soon," Billy said.

"And Mr. Abner?"

Billy pointed far off to the corn stubble, where Abner's tractor pulled the disk. He stayed clear of people until just before game time; then his tall figure and dusty cap appeared in the back of the crowd. Manuel González squinted off to the field, shrugged and turned to unload their little grill and supper things. Billy wished Abner and Manuel would talk, like Mavis and María, but so far the two men had barely spoken.

"Okay, Farm Team, let's loosen up with some short catch," Aaron Goldberg called. "We'll take infield in a half hour or so."

Billy joined the others and began to lob the ball back and forth with Jesús González. Neither of them spoke; neither wanted to be first to speak. Jesús's eyes fell to Billy's new glove, but he would not give Billy the satisfaction of commenting upon it. If Jesús wanted to play that game, neither would Billy tell him about it.

But finally Billy had to say something. He was, after all, the host. "So, when do you have to go back to Mexico?"

"Soon. Maybe tomorrow. Papa doesn't tell us much."

"Like my old man," Billy said, glancing to the far-off sound of Abner's tractor.

Jesús shrugged and tossed the ball back to Billy.

"How far is it, to Mexico?"

"Forty hours or four flat tires, whichever comes first."

Billy glanced at the station wagon. "You drive straight through?"

Jesús spit neatly to the side. "No. We stay at Holiday Inns."

Billy stared.

"With pool and room service," Jesús added sarcastically, tossing the ball harder this time.

Billy whipped the ball back equally fast. Jesús had his father's edge of anger about him. It was like a sharp knife in a thin sheath, always threatening to break through and cut someone.

"We try to drive straight through," Jesús answered finally. "Nobody wants wetbacks camping in their town."

Billy was silent for a while as they tossed and caught. He tried another direction. "What about school? You have to go back to school soon?"

"You think we don't have schools in Mexico?" Jesús said, spinning for a sharp relay to Billy.

"I thought all you did down there was play baseball," Billy answered.

Jesús actually grinned, then bounced a hard one at Billy's ankles. He fielded cleanly and returned the favor. Then they began to fire the ball at each other as hard as they could.

"Hey!" Coach Goldberg barked at them. "How about saving something for the game? We start at seven."

As the Farm Team loosened up, cars one by one turned into the Baggs farm and followed the directions of General Ole. At summer's end many of the tourists had already gone home, and most farmers were busy with harvest, so attendance was noticeably down. Still, thirty cars soon sat neatly parked alongside the field. A small queue of people gathered at the corncrib concession stand. It was staffed by the Lutheran Ladies' Aid, and from it came the smells of coffee and hot dogs. A gaggle of small barefooted kids raced and shrieked among the rows of cars. Old men leaned here and there on the plank fence as hunched and still as old trees, except for the intermittent spurts of chewing tobacco that sailed off suddenly, like brown grasshoppers. Cicadas buzzed sharply from the windbreak, and a faint haze of golden dust rose above the farm, softening the sharp outlines of barns and machinery. At ground level the earth held the flatter scents of the coming season—a hint, around an old gopher burrow, of cooler air. As Billy reached low for a stray ball, he bent to get it in summer and stood up in autumn. He stared at the ball. Then looked about him for long moments—at the farm, at the whole scene. He wished Robert was here; wished he could see all this.

"*Que?*" Jesús called.

Billy blinked. "*Nada,*" he said, and threw a long strike back to Jesús.

Creating more dust was the small caravan of Town Team cars led by the Kenwoods' Cadillac convertible, Mark Kenwood at the wheel. Beside him was his wife, wearing dark sunglasses and a Jackie Kennedy–like scarf tied over her hair. King was not in the car, though Butch Redbird was. He held up both arms in greeting to the crowd as if he was the president of the United States. Billy had to grin; since Butch was King's favorite catcher, Butch was not above getting a few favors in return, especially from Mark Kenwood. Following the white Cadillac was Coach Anderson's battered little Toyota (no King there, either). Bringing up the rear was a heavy Olds 88 chock-full of girls. Billy thought he saw, inside the car, a glint of platinum hair.

Butch Redbird made a grand entrance by hopping over the side of the Cadillac before it stopped, then turning to bow before it. "I love this car!" he called to Billy. "Gonna have me one someday."

"No doubt about it," Billy called back.

"Hello, Billy," Coach Anderson said from his window. He got out and came forward; a second man in a baseball cap, a stopwatch around his neck, accompanied him.

"Evening, Coach," Billy said, coming over to shake hands. He kept looking past the coach to the Olds 88, as brown-legged girls emerged one after another. The longest and shiniest legs belonged to Suzy.

"Billy, this is Mr. Bob LaMott, a college friend of mine who coaches baseball over at North Dakota State University."

"Howdy," Billy said, shaking hands briefly.

"Heard a lot about you, son," Mr. LaMott said.

Billy nodded absently; he was looking beyond, to the girls.

"Well, good luck tonight," Mr. LaMott said.

"Sure," Billy said. Suzy waved to Billy, a small, tight wave. "Excuse me," Billy said, and walked toward her. As he approached Suzy, he reminded himself that this was his turf, his ground; he had no reason to act stupid.

Then King Kenwood stepped from the Oldsmobile. Billy halted; his smile faded. The town girls and Kenwood gathered in a small knot as they looked around. "Hicksville," someone murmured, and there were giggles. Billy stiffened. Suzy quickly separated herself from the group and came over to Billy.

"Told you I'd come," she said.

"Hello, Suzy," he said evenly, trying as usual, when he first saw her again, not to melt down or freeze up inside. "Welcome to Hicksville."

"I'm sorry," she said quickly, glancing over her shoulder at the town kids. "They need to get out more—including King."

Billy shrugged. "At least you came," he said. His gaze flickered to Kenwood, who was staring at the man with Coach Anderson. King could spot a baseball coach at five hundred yards.

"Unfortunately, I don't know how long the other girls will want to stay," she added, glancing apologetically at her watch.

"How about you?" Billy said.

She paused. "How long would you like me to stay?"

They were silent; a current arced between them.

"As long as you can," Billy said. Beyond them, King Kenwood looked torn between interrupting Suzy and Billy and going to see who was with Coach Anderson. Luckily, King's father called him over. "Let's go, King; start loosening up!"

"Anyway, I told the girls you might show them around the farm," Suzy said.

"There are some new kittens in the hayloft," Billy replied. He could have kicked himself. It was a line he planned to use later with Suzy, alone.

"Kittens? I'm sure they'd love to see them."

While King was occupied with his father, who helped him stretch, Billy led the girls away. He went first up the ladder through the narrow doorway, moving his bale hook to one side so that no one would get poked by it, then standing by to make sure no one fell from the ladder. Suzy reached up; Billy caught her hand and pulled her into the dim loft. "Thank you," she said. Her fingers were long and firm, her hand warm.

Jennifer and three other town girls stepped gingerly into the loft. One of them sneezed, then kept her hand over her face. "My allergies are going to shit!"

"Listen!" Suzy said and cocked her head.

They were all quiet.

From a dark crevice deep in the stacks of bales came faint mewing.

"Ooooo," Suzy cooed, and she hurried forward. Billy pulled away a half dozen bales, and finally uncovered the nest of calico kittens. Already each as big as a fist, their eyes clear and open, the brightly colored kittens scrambled here and there over mouse skeletons and pigeon carcasses as they burrowed against each other or tried to escape. One runty one moved much slower than the rest, as sluggish as if it was underwater. Suzy retrieved it.

"Oh, they're darling," the girls cooed. Billy watched as each girl held one.

"Which one's your favorite?" Suzy asked, holding the watery-eyed runt.

"I dunno," Billy said. In truth, he didn't care one way or another about the barn cats. There were several litters every year. Only a few kittens survived, so he tried not to get attached to any one in particular.

"I like this one," Suzy said, coming closer to Billy, holding out the runt.

"That one probably won't make it," Billy said.

"Make it?" Suzy said. The girls all turned to look at Billy.

"Through the winter, I meant," he said. Silence fell in the hayloft. "Then again, who knows? Maybe it will grow," Billy added quickly.

The other girls resumed their petting and cooing. "Listen," he said to Suzy, "I've got to go warm up."

"Okay," Suzy said. "Do you mind if we stay up here for a while?"

"No, go ahead," Billy said. "There's also a

swing." He pointed to the old knotted rope that hung from the rafters.

"A swing! A swing!" the girls exclaimed.

"Me first!" Suzy called. She set down the kitten and raced forward.

As Billy climbed down from the loft, his image was of Suzy Langen, her long brown legs wrapped around the rope, her ponytail streaming behind as she pumped herself through the pale green light.

Back in the full sunshine of the evening, Aaron Goldberg was leading the Farm Team through infield practice, rapping the baseball to the various positions. King was warming on the sidelines, making the ball pop in Butch's glove; Mark Kenwood stood nearby watching.

"Where the hell have you been?" Aaron said to Billy.

"Brief roll in the hay?" Gina added.

"I was showing the girls the barn cats," Billy said, quickly grabbing his glove from the bench.

"Town girls and barn cats. Hard to tell who's who," Gina said sarcastically.

"What do you know about it?" Billy said.

"Enough to know those Green Lawn babes ain't your type," Gina replied.

"So what is my type?" Billy said crabbily.

"It sure ain't them," Gina said.

"Let's focus on baseball, shall we?" Aaron said in his big coach's voice. He looked around. "Where the hell is Heather?"

Gina nodded to the concession stand. "She's in

with the old ladies, giving her kid a suck."

Some of the boys laughed. Aaron sighed. "A nursing catcher. It's one of those things they don't teach in coaching clinics," he muttered.

With Heather back catching and the Town Team taking infield, Billy warmed up his pitching arm. Aaron, chewing a spear of alfalfa hay, watched him. "Throw over the top," he advised.

"Right, Coach," Billy muttered. Unfortunately, Aaron was always right about baseball. Watching King's perfect, smooth motion helped Billy find his own delivery. He made himself concentrate on throwing mechanics as he listened to the faint sound of the girls shrieking in the hayloft. Suzy's laughter rose above the rest, and he bounced a pitch in the dirt, which Heather blocked expertly.

"Billy's got kitty on his mind," Gina remarked. The players on the Farm Team bench snickered.

"Calico, to be exact," Billy said. He grooved the next pitch, which slapped hard in Heather's glove.

Gina smirked at Aaron. "What's your favorite color?"

"I'm color blind," Aaron replied.

The Farm Team cracked up.

"What? I am. I really am color blind," he protested.

"That means he likes them all," Shawn added.

Gina giggled, and the remarks from the bench degenerated quickly. "Keep it clean," Aaron said in his official voice. In the middle of Billy's windup came more squeals of teenage girls in the hayloft; his pitch soared six feet over Heather's head. "I got a feeling it's going to be a long night," she sighed, trotting after the ball.

The Farm Team, being home, took the field first. The coach from North Dakota had volunteered to call balls and strikes. He stared as Heather Erickson brought out a straw bale and propped it upright behind the plate. "Could I ask . . . ?" he began.

Heather squatted behind the bale. "For Billy's fastball," she said. "I ain't gonna get killed; I'm a nursing mother."

"I think it's a hazard," Mark Kenwood called out. "It shouldn't be on the field."

"Let's see how it works, first," Coach LaMott said evenly.

Heather popped out to retrieve Billy's first warm-up pitch, a high heater that thumped a puff of golden dust from the bale. "You'll thank me for it, too," she said to the ump.

"Unofficial game, unofficial rules—the bale stays," the ump announced.

"Nanner, nanner, nanner," Gina called across to Mark Kenwood.

After a few more warm-up pitches, Bob LaMott announced, "Balls in, coming down."

"Balls in, coming down!" Heather echoed. She received the ball, stepped out and nailed the second-base bag.

"She should catch for us," King called, and the Town Team players laughed. Heather blushed.

Billy rubbed up the ball, took the rubber, then

fired. He shut down the first three batters on nine fastballs. With each pitch Bob LaMott showed less of himself outside the perimeter of the straw bale. "Stee-rike three!" he called on the last batter. Glancing into the stands as he trotted off, Billy caught his father's eyes; Abner nodded slightly to Billy. The coach from North Dakota hoisted his umpire's mask and turned to raise both eyebrows at Coach Anderson, who grinned widely and pumped his arm once.

"Hey—whose side are you on?" Tiny Tim Loren chirped at Coach Anderson.

In the bottom of the inning Gina Erickson led off. King Kenwood, on the mound for the Town Team, stared down at her.

"Whatsa matter, never seen a girl lead off before?" Gina called.

King wound up. On the first pitch Gina squared around and laid down a bunt, surprising everyone. The ball hopped along like a sick chicken with sunstroke, then died just inside the foul line. By the time King bare-handed the ball to first base, Gina was standing on the bag, pretending to pick her nose. The small crowd clapped.

"It's all in the coaching," Aaron said to Billy.

"Right, sure," Billy replied dryly.

King, his back to the plate, rubbed up the ball for a good long time.

Raúl González batted second and rapped a sharp single up the middle, but the center fielder gunned down Gina, who stupidly tried to advance to third.

Jesús batted next and sacrificed Raúl to second. Billy, batting fourth, now faced King Kenwood.

The two stared at each other. Voices in the stands quieted. King whistled his first pitch an inch off Billy's belt buckle. Billy tried to crush the ball and missed it cleanly. He took a called strike two on the outside corner, then swung mightily at a fat-looking pitch dead over the center of the plate. Trouble was, the ball arrived about a minute later than Billy's bat: change-up.

"Keep your weight back next time," Aaron said as Billy kicked dust on his return to the bench.

"I know, I know," Billy grumbled.

"Let's go!" Abner called to Billy with impatience in his voice.

In the top half of the second inning it was Billy on the mound facing King, who batted clean-up. He glared down at Kenwood. Voices and chatter in the stands quieted. Billy's first fastball hummed just under Kenwood's jaw—chin music. King coolly bent backward from the waist without moving his feet from the box.

"Good pitch, good pitch," Abner called.

Billy took a huge windup and threw his next heater behind Kenwood, who dove for cover.

"He's going to kill somebody!" Mark Kenwood shouted. King got up, dusted himself off, then took several steps toward the mound.

"Time!" the umpire called. Coach Anderson trotted onto the field, got between King and Billy.

"Now I know you two are not bosom buddies,

but let's not get hurt out here. I need you both on the school team this spring, all right?"

Billy and King nodded begrudgingly.

"Now get back in there and play baseball," the coach said. He pushed them in opposite directions.

Once back on the mound, Billy could not find the strike zone.

"He's wild, he's wild!" Mark Kenwood shouted. Sure enough, Billy walked Kenwood. Then he gave a free pass to Tiny Tim, whose strike zone was the size of a milk carton. Tim did cartwheels all the way to first base, drawing applause and laughter from the crowd. Billy was not amused. Bearing down, he struck out the next two batters on six pitches, then walked the next two. One run in, bases loaded.

Aaron Goldberg finally called "Time!" and trotted to the mound. He glanced around at the bases, all occupied, then leaned in close to Billy. "Do you think Gina is too young for me?"

"Huh?" Billy said.

"Gina—is she too young? I mean, you know, like jailbait?"

Billy stared down at him. He put his hands on his hips. "You're supposed to be out here saying things to me like 'Hey, Billy, just throw strikes, keep the ball low, one more out,' that kind of stuff," he said indignantly.

"Right . . ." Aaron said absently, smiling over his shoulder at Gina.

Billy booted Aaron off the mound, then fanned the next batter on three smoking fastballs. Back at the bench he tossed down his glove. "Some coach you are," he muttered.

"Thank you very much," Aaron said with a wink to the rest of his team.

However, even the managerial magic of Coach Goldberg could not save Billy from himself. Suzy Langen had come down from the hayloft to watch the game and now stood behind the Farm Team bench; Billy could not help looking her way between pitches. Finally, in the third inning, Aaron came to the mound again. "Six strikeouts and seven walks," he said to Billy. "This is not your night."

"Maybe, maybe not," Billy murmured, glancing past Aaron to the fence line where Suzy stood, watching.

"That's it!" Aaron said decisively, and took the ball from Billy's hand. Billy gave it up without a fight. Mark Kenwood clapped loudly.

"Jesús?" Aaron called. Jesús González trotted forward.

Sweating slightly, Billy took a seat on the bench near Suzy. "I couldn't hit the broad side of a barn tonight," Billy muttered, trying to put on a disgusted face.

"Next time," Suzy said.

"Next summer, you mean. This is the last Farm Team game."

"Really?" Suzy said, looking disappointed.

"Yup," Billy said. They held each other's gaze for a long moment.

The sound of a car departing turned Billy's gaze.

It was the Oldsmobile full of girls.

"Your ride," Billy said.

Suzy shrugged. "They had to get back to town."

"But how are you getting back?" he asked stupidly.

"I'll catch a lift with Doug's sister. Or someone."

They were silent. Jesús threw a strike. "By the way, the kittens were very successful," she said.

"It's the standard tour for city folks," Billy said.

Suzy smiled. "I love calicoes."

"You should take one home."

"Really?" Suzy said.

"Sure. There are way too many, which means they'll probably get distemper or else I'll have to get rid of some of them before winter sets in."

Suzy drew back slightly. "Get rid of them? You mean it?"

Billy shrugged apologetically. He looked back to the game.

"How?" Suzy said.

"Drown them in a gunny sack. Knock them on the head, whatever," he said. "On the farm, cats come and cats go, so if you took one—or more— that would be good."

"Maybe I should go look at them again," she said.

Billy turned to stare at her. "Want me to come?"

She smiled. Then her eyes flickered across to King Kenwood, who watched them from the Town Team's bench.

"What about him?" Billy said.

"King's trying to impress that guy from North Dakota," Suzy said. "He'll never miss us."

"I'll meet you there in three minutes," Billy whispered.

After Suzy disappeared, Billy pretended interest in the game. Then he took a brief look over his shoulder for his mother, who was chatting with María González, and for his father. Abner was leaning on the fence; he and Manuel González were smoking small black cigars. Perfect. During some sudden cheering, when a ball went bounding to the outfield, Billy slipped away.

In the dim, sweet-smelling loft the light was duskier now, and the cheers from the ball field were faint and far away. Suzy and Billy looked, then listened for the kittens. Not being stupid, they had disappeared deep into the hay bale maze and made not a peep.

"Sometimes they hide," Billy said. "They'll come out after a while."

They stood next to each other in the dim, towering loft. "It's so quiet," Suzy said.

Billy, truly alone with Suzy for the first time, stood as mute and dumb as a barn wall. His eyes went to the tattered old rope swing. "Swing?"

"Push me?" Suzy said. Billy nodded. They climbed the bales to the square green cliff, and there, with one hand on his shoulder, Suzy leaned on Billy as he fit her foot in the bottom loop.

"Ready?"

She nodded, then giggled briefly as Billy swung

her away from the platform. When she came back, Billy caught her at the hips and pushed her again.

"Higher," she said.

Billy obeyed, and soon she flowed back and forth across the space in longer and longer arcs. She arched backward, hanging on with only one hand. "From Brazil, the famous trapeze artist, Conchita!" she said, trying to keep her voice low.

One part of Billy understood that there were certain images that once seen, burned themselves—like photographs—inside the brain like a tattoo on skin. Another part of him did not think at all, but only caught her and sent her away again, drinking in, over and over, the warm wash of her scent. "Enough!" she finally called, laughing, and Billy caught her and steadied her on the bales.

They stood there.

"We could both go," she said; he was still holding on to her hips.

"Okay."

"How do we do it?" she asked.

"I don't know—I've never gone with anybody—on the swing, I mean," he added quickly.

Suzy laughed, then looked upward into the darkness. "Will the rope hold us?"

"Absolutely," Billy replied.

"Okay," she said, "so you put your foot in the loop first."

Billy obeyed.

"Now me, on top."

"Now what?" Billy said.

"I suppose we have to hold on to each other," she said softly.

"I guess." And they did. "Ready?" Billy said.

"Count of three?" Suzy added.

They counted and pushed off. Both of them shrieked and grabbed each other tighter to keep from falling. They ended up with legs intertwined, her face in his neck, his face in her hair. "We forgot one thing," Suzy said as they coasted.

"What's that?"

"There's no one to push us."

"So we have to pump," Billy said. At the end of the first arc they leaned into each other and pushed with their legs.

"Yes!" Suzy said, as they gained a little height and momentum.

At the opposite end they pushed again. Swinging, however, cannot be hurried, and they had to find the best rhythm, and the best rhythm was slow and steady.

With each swing they went a little higher and held on to each other a little tighter. After several arcs he took a breath, then kissed the side of her hair; she wrapped herself tighter around him. Only the hard, straight cord of the rope kept them apart.

"Mmmmm," she breathed against him, and they kept pumping. Billy's leg was inside her thighs; he could feel their firmness, their heat, and he was certain she could feel his own, but she did not shy away from him, and they continued their slowly rising arc across the hayloft.

Pump and coast.

Pump and coast.

Pump and coast.

After a few minutes her breathing came faster, as if she was getting frightened. "You all right?" he asked.

"Higher. Let's go higher," she murmured, and buried her face tighter against his neck.

Billy obliged. Soon they were soaring clear across the great breadth of the loft, melted against each other. At the very highest part of their arc Suzy suddenly said, "Oh, Billy!" and did something— either let go, or tried to stop, or tried to get away from him—a sudden lurching of her body.

"It's okay—I've got you!" Billy called. As he grabbed on tighter to keep from losing her, their rhythm was lost and the swing began to buck crazily, dangerously. Then, in the dimness above them, with a sharp tearing sound, the rope broke.

Before either of them could make a sound, the hayloft floor—luckily covered with a foot of alfalfa chaff and dust—leaped up and slammed them. *Unnnk-thwump!* Their bodies thudded and rolled once, and then they were lying tangled up with one another.

"Suzy?" Billy groaned.

"I'm okay, I think," she breathed. "You?"

"Breath—knocked—out—" Billy wheezed.

She rolled to her knees and bent over him. He looked up at her with a helpless, frozen look as he waited for air to come.

"Billy! Are you sure?"

He nodded reassuringly, then finally got his breath. He began to gasp and spit green alfalfa dust.

"Can you move?" she asked.

"Sure." He didn't feel like it just yet.

"Anything broken?"

"No. How about you?"

"Luckily I landed on top of you."

Billy sat up and squinted above him at the broken rope, which still swayed in the shadows. "I guess the two of us were too heavy," he said.

"No kidding." She reached over and wiped something from his forehead.

"What happened?" Billy said, bringing his gaze back to Suzy. "I thought you were falling or something," he added, remembering her puzzling behavior at the height of their swinging.

"Or something," she said, and put a finger across his lips. She smiled, not a big smile but a soft one, a smile like he'd never seen any girl smile before. Billy suddenly pulled her back in the soft, loose hay, and then they were kissing. They kissed hard for a long time, until they had to stop for air. Afterward they just lay there, breathing against each other.

Then Billy moved his left hand down her back. She let him. He moved it tentatively under her blouse and onto her bare skin. "Mmmm," she murmured. Billy stroked her back for a long time. She stirred against his hand, moving with it. Billy withdrew his hand and traced it down the side of her face to her neck. She leaned closer against him. Billy, holding his breath, let his hand slide lower, onto the front of her blouse, then stopped. "It's okay," she whispered. He traced the soft, firm rise of her curves, ever so slowly pausing with his fingertips on the first button of her blouse. "Okay?" He asked this time, and by way of answer she kissed his neck. Billy moved his fingers to the second button, then the third, opening each one, and then cupped the silky taut fabric of her bra. "Are you sure?" he whispered. She didn't stop him. Soon he had opened her entire blouse. In one motion she buried his face in the warm rise of her breasts, then pushed him away. "No—we're going too fast," she said suddenly.

"I'm sorry," Billy began.

"It's okay. I wanted to. And you asked." She leaned back in the shadows and quickly buttoned her blouse.

He watched her.

"What?" she said. She was smiling; her teeth shone in the dusky light.

He was about say something—what, he was not sure, but it had the word "love" somewhere in it—when a voice came from below.

"Suzy? Suzy, where are you?"

They looked up. Suzy stiffened, and her eyes widened. It was King, coming up the hayloft ladder.

"Well well," King said, as he surveyed the two of them.

The way he said it, flatly, without heat, made Suzy step backward. "King, it's not what you think," she said.

"So what is it, then?"

"Nothing, King!"

"It doesn't look like nothing," King said, eyes on Billy. His gaze went to the hand-sized hay hook that hung on the wall; it shone dully, curving like a great fish hook. He swung his dark eyes back to Billy and slowly reached out for the steel tool.

Suzy shrank back. "King, my God, don't!"

Billy felt his blood flow to the edges of him, to his fists and feet. He readied himself.

"Stay away from her!" King said hoarsely. With a whistling sweep the hook flashed in front of Billy. It was meant to be a warning shot, not a killing blow, but Billy, in the soft layer of alfalfa chaff, lost a half second of reaction time. As he jerked backward the hook caught his shirt and tore away its front, and the tip burned across his chest.

King stared at the tool in his hand.

Billy stared at his ripped T-shirt. His best one. He suddenly swore, lunged at King, got inside his reach, and caught Kenwood's arm. He wrenched it backward. Kenwood groaned, and the hay hook tumbled far off, out of sight and harmless in the hay dust. Now they faced each other, King holding his shoulder, Billy holding his hand across his burning chest, then lurched at each other. They flailed, grunted, shouted, kicked, swore. Suzy stood frozen, watching them beat on each other. Billy and King rolled in the choking, coarse dust. Then Billy heard Suzy clambering down the ladder and calling, "Help, help—they're killing each other!"

Back at the field the game halted. Billy and King, noses bloody and shirts ripped, were pushed toward the crowd by Coach Anderson and Mavis Baggs. Gina, glaring at Suzy, brought up the rear. Team members gathered around their respective warriors. A rustling and muttering snaked through the players like a fire in prairie grass. "Rumble time," Heather said, and picked up a baseball bat. The González brothers turned for their hoes still strapped atop their station wagon. The coach from North Dakota ducked for his car.

"Unless you're on deck to bat, put down the damn wood," Coach Anderson shouted.

"Yeah—back off, all of you!" called Butch Redbird. He seemed as angry as the coach. Manuel González spit a stream of high-octane Spanish at his boys, who shamefacedly froze in their tracks. Around the two fighters bats wavered, then clattered to the ground.

"Look at you two, look at you two," was all Mavis could say, fighting back tears. Mrs. Kenwood, keening low in her throat as if her son was dead, had slumped against her husband. Mark Kenwood could not let her go, or she would topple to the ground. Billy could see King mainly from one eye; the other was closing, swelling shut as steadily as the sun going down. King's lower lip was swollen like a hot dog ready to burst.

"Who started this?" Abner Baggs thundered.

Neither boy would speak or look up.

"I've got a damn bullwhip in the barn," Abner said.

"Easy, Abner, easy," the coach said, stepping forward. "Maybe I should handle this."

Mavis nodded quickly and restrained Abner.

"King, honey, are you injured?" his mother said, coming forward and trying to hug him.

King winced and pushed her away. "Just my arm," he muttered.

"If his pitching arm is hurt, I'll sue you to king-dom come!" Mark Kenwood shouted at Abner Baggs. "You can kiss this farm good-bye."

"I'll tell you what you can kiss," Abner said, stepping forward and grabbing at Mark.

"Enough of that," the coach commanded, pushing Abner and Mark apart. Billy had never seen the coach so angry.

"How did it happen, honey? How did he hit you?" King's mother asked.

"Who says he hit me?" King said hoarsely.

Heads turned.

"Well, just what were you doing if not fighting?" the coach asked, hands on hips.

"I fell," King mumbled.

"You fell," the coach said.

King nodded.

Attention turned to Billy, who was attempting to hold the tatters of his T-shirt over his scored, red-streaked chest.

"And you? What happened to you?" Coach Anderson asked.

Billy shrugged. "I fell, too. Against a nail."

Abner swore under his breath.

"Both of you fell in the hayloft," the coach said.

Billy and King glanced sideways at each other. They nodded.

"May I ask what were you doing in the hayloft in the first place?" Mavis said sharply. "You were supposed to be playing baseball."

The two boys were silent.

"I can probably explain," Suzy said, stepping forward. "Billy said there were extra barn cats, and I could have a kitten if I wanted, so he took me up there to look for one."

People stared at her.

"Then King came up and thought, well, I don't know," Suzy said, blushing, "that something was going on between Billy and me."

There were snickers from the Farm Team, and some from the Town Team. "That must be when you fell, too," Gina said. She stepped forward to flick an alfalfa stalk from Suzy's hair. "A hard fall. So hard the buttons on your blouse got mixed up."

Every eye went to Suzy's blouse. The top button-hole was free; below, at her waist, was an extra button and an extra inch of white cotton. Farm Team and most of Town Team erupted in laughter; even some of the adults could not hold back. Suzy's face turned scarlet, and she froze in place. Eyes bored in on her, particularly those of Mr. and Mrs. Kenwood. Billy tried to stand, tried to move toward Suzy, but none of his limbs obeyed.

Suddenly Butch Redbird pushed through the crowd. "Come on!" he said to Suzy. He grabbed her wrist and made a pathway for her escape. The spectators, chuckling, began to disperse as well. "Just a couple of young bucks locking horns over a doe," an old farmer remarked.

"Maybe so, but there are other ways than fighting to resolve problems," said Mavis. She glared down at the boys.

"I agree," Coach Anderson said. He addressed Billy and King. "School is starting soon. You boys fight there, you soon won't be in school—and you sure as hell won't be on my baseball team come spring."

Billy and King shifted their eyes up to the coach, then to each other.

"Now shake hands and call it quits," the coach said.

Both King and Billy set their jaws and looked down; neither moved.

"I asked you to shake hands," the coach repeated ominously.

"You heard him," Mark Kenwood said suddenly to King.

The remaining spectators fell silent. King and Billy remained motionless.

"All right, game's over," the coach said, with a decisive sweep of his arm.

"What? It's tied!" players from both teams called. "We can't just stop."

"We just did," the coach said. "Town Team, load up the gear."

There were groans of disappointment from both sides.

"See what fighting can do?" Mavis said to Billy. "It ruins things for everybody."

Billy was unmoved. "See you in school," he whispered hoarsely to Kenwood.

"I'll be waiting," Kenwood breathed. Holding his shoulder, he limped toward the cars.

"If he lays a hand on my son, your probation officer's gonna hear about it," said Mark Kenwood to Abner. "And you'll end up in the slammer again— I guarantee it."

"And when I get out, I'll bring my goddamn

Caterpillar to your house next time," Abner growled.

"That's enough!" Coach Anderson said. He shook his head, then took off his baseball cap and ran a hand through his hair.

Mavis turned to Billy. "You get in the house and get cleaned up," she said.

"Should he see a doctor?" Aaron ventured.

"I'll doctor his ass with my whip," Abner said, pushing Billy forward. Billy took the hint and moved.

"There are better ways than another beating," the coach said.

"That's all this family knows," Mark Kenwood remarked.

"So what are they, *Coach*?" Abner said, doing his best to ignore Mark Kenwood.

"I'm thinking, Abner, I'm thinking."

Billy came out of the shower, his cuts stinging, the pain in his muscles beginning to swell and throb like gathering storm clouds. He limped to the porch screen door and peered out. The field was empty, the parking lot nearly so; he hadn't gotten a chance to say good-bye to Aaron, to the González family, to anyone. His eyes continued to scan the yard. The only cars left were the coach's Toyota and the white Cadillac. King slouched in the backseat.

He squinted closer. By the field, at one end of a pine bench, sat Abner and Mavis; on the other end sat King's parents. Before them stood the coach, gesturing sharply to one pair, then to the other.

"I've never seen the coach so pissed," Butch said.

Billy started. Butch was sitting on the steps.

"Where's Suzy?" Billy said.

"She caught a lift back to town with Doug's sister."

Billy was silent.

"Bad scene, man," Butch said, still looking over to the coach.

"What's he saying?" Billy asked.

"I don't know, but it ain't pretty."

Just before morning Billy dreamed he was covered with heavy stones at the bottom of an avalanche. He was pinned. Sharp rocks pressed down on every muscle. Then his alarm went off, and he sat up—and the crunched, crushed feeling didn't go away. Every muscle from his face to his calves ached as if he was a bull rider who had been dragged through the rodeo ring and stomped on. When he stood up, he remained bent like an old man. Pulling on his clothes, he groaned each time he lifted an arm or a leg. Mavis was waiting for him at the bottom of the stairs.

"So, Mr. Tough Guy, how do you feel?" She was not smiling.

"Fine, Ma," Billy said quickly. He winced as he tried to stand up straighter.

"Good, because I've got a few extra chores I'd like done today." She handed him a list as long as his hand, and in small writing, too.

"Sure, Ma, no problem." Clenching his teeth to keep from groaning, Billy bent to pull on his work boots.

"Since it's Saturday, I'll be around to see that you get them all done," Mavis added.

Billy glanced at the kitchen clock. Five-thirty A.M. It was going to be a long day. Crossing the yard, he glanced around for his Jim Kaat glove, missing since last night. He didn't dare look for it now.

Abner was already in the barn when he got there but did not greet him. Not a good sign.

They worked silently, Billy pushing the feed cart and carrying buckets of grain, Abner following with a smaller pail of salt and minerals. Billy could feel Abner's eyes on him. Soon they set about the milking. Abner chewed slowly on a long yellow spike of straw. Billy kept sneaking looks at his father. His father continued staring his peculiar stare, the one that sometimes looked almost like a smile. Billy wished his father would just explode at him as usual—jerk him around by his shirt, cuss him out, threaten to tan his hide—be done with it.

After the last cow was milked, Abner finally spoke. "Turn the cows out, then meet me in the milk house," he said.

Billy obeyed. "Hiee, get going," he muttered as he knocked open the wooden stanchions and shooed the big Holsteins toward the door; if his legs had not ached so badly, he would have kicked each cow in the ass. Soon the barn was empty, and he had no choice but to enter the milk house.

A barn stool awaited him. His father stood at the stainless steel sink, elbow deep in soapy water as he slowly scrubbed a big silvery kettle.

"Sit down," Abner said, and gestured to the stool. Soap bubbles spattered to the floor with the faint smell of chlorine.

Billy obeyed. His father worked on. Behind Billy was the bulk tank; the slow, dull churning of its paddle sounded like waves, and the escaping heat felt good on his back.

Finally Abner turned. "I know, from experience, that what you're going through ain't easy."

"What am I going through?" Billy muttered.

"Puberty," Abner said. "The big change. Whatever you want to call it."

Billy was silent.

"I know, from experience, that it makes a man crazy. As crazy as a bull with a belly full of loco weed."

Billy waited.

"And you're probably wondering why I haven't said anything about the girl you happen to be loco over."

Billy swallowed.

"Well, I only last night found out who it was," Abner began.

"You mean Ma didn't tell you earlier?" Billy asked quickly.

"No," Abner said, with a passing dark look.

Billy was silent. Come to think of it, last night he had heard loud voices arguing downstairs, but he'd thought he was dreaming about his own fight with King.

"Anyway, my first thought was this: Why, with all the girls in Flint, with all the girls in the whole damn county, why does her name have to be Langen?"

Billy hardened his gaze, looked down.

"The daughter of the judge who rode roughshod over this family when your brother was killed," his father continued, "like . . . like we were so much horseshit in the dirt."

Billy stared at the floor, at the drain where a trickle of water swirled out of sight and into the ground below. "Robert is dead," he mumbled.

His father jerked his head around to Billy. "What did you say?"

"I said, Robert is dead." He spoke clearly this time.

Abner's forehead furrowed in sudden, paralyzed anger.

"But I'm not," Billy said, seizing the moment. "I deserve a life, dammit!"

Abner appeared to count to ten. Then he said, "That's true."

Billy's mouth dropped open with surprise. He had expected, in the least, a blow upside the head. Abner turned to stare out the window. His eyes took on that faraway gleam, the same look he'd had when he had climbed aboard his old Caterpillar and headed toward Randy Meyers's car lot.

"Anyway, I thought on it late last night, I mean

the matter of you sniffing around the Langen girl. And I reached a decision."

"Which is?" Billy said sarcastically.

Abner turned. "Go to it."

Billy blinked.

"I'm not gonna stand in your way," his father said. He returned to the sink and his work.

Billy cocked his head. "Why . . . after what you just said . . . why wouldn't you?"

Abner laughed once, a short croaking chuckle. "Because my son is fooling with his daughter? It serves old man Langen right."

Billy stared. He felt his heartbeat begin to thud angrily in his ears.

"Just don't go too far with her," Abner said, continuing his washing. "You know what I mean. Fooling around with her is one thing. Marrying her is another."

"Wait a minute," Billy said. His voice trembled. He had to think hard to find even the simplest words. "You think I'm . . . using her to get back at her father?"

"I didn't say that. But if that's the result, it works for me."

Billy's hands began to shake. "What kind of . . . what kind of—" he began hoarsely, but rage choked off his words.

"What kind of father am I?" Abner finished. He looked at Billy. "The only one you got, so you may as well get used to it."

Billy lurched to his feet. "What if . . . what if I

don't want to get used to it anymore?" His eyes suddenly burned with hot, angry, salty water.

Abner's hands went still in the sink. "Don't play hardball with me. You do, and you'll be looking for somewhere else to hang your hat."

Billy wanted to scream at Abner: *Then who would do the chores? Who would clean the gutter and the calf pens? Who would feed silage and bale hay? Who would cut firewood and chop it? Who would do all the other shit work around here? Where would you find a slave like me?* But he didn't. He felt suddenly exhausted, beaten down, flattened, run over. He wiped his eyes. "Anything else?" he said dumbly.

"There is one more thing," Abner said. "You and that Kenwood boy? Coach Anderson came up with a plan to keep you two from killing each other. I'm not wild about it, but his parents and your mother and I agreed to give it a try."

"Do I have a say in it?" Billy asked woodenly.

"No," Abner replied.

For his first day of school, Billy came downstairs to breakfast dressed in his old jeans, black T-shirt and scuffed cowboy boots. Mavis stopped to stare.

"Where are your new school clothes?" she asked.

Abner stopped a bite of pancake midway between plate and mouth; he swung his gaze to Billy.

"They don't feel right," Billy muttered, taking his seat at the table.

"I washed them, I ironed them, we made sure they fit," Mavis said. Her hands went to her hips; her eyes narrowed.

Billy shrugged. "I'm not wearin' them."

"You mean to tell me we spent—" Abner began loudly, rattling down his fork.

"No, take it easy," Mavis murmured to Abner. "We don't have to discuss this right now."

"They just feel stupid," Billy said of his clothes. "School feels stupid," he added, and bent to his food.

Abner's jaw began to move, but Mavis hushed him with a rapid shake of the pancake turner.

In the raw, low sunlight, Billy waited for the orange bus. A robin, perched atop a fence post, waited with him. He wished the damn bird could take his place in school. Then again, today was his chance to see Suzy.

And King Kenwood.

Scowling, Billy reached underneath his T-shirt and scratched the narrow scab across his chest. Soon came the far-off rumble and dust of the school bus. He straightened his spine and got ready. First-day-of-school butterflies never went away, he supposed. Dust rolled closer, and brakes groaned and squeaked as the bus lurched to a stop; its accordion-fold door jerked sideways, and from inside came the usual hoots and hollers. Billy settled into a seat beside Gina Erickson, who was wearing way too much makeup for the first day of school, plus high heels. Gina had this thing about being short.

"Hey, didn't your ma buy you new school clothes?" she asked.

Billy nodded.

"So why ain't you wearing them?"

"I didn't feel like it," Billy answered. He looked her up and down. "What's that smell?"

"My new perfume," Gina said brightly.

"No kidding," Billy said, squinting his eyes and fanning the air around him. His eyes began to water.

"Rose Blossom. Got it at the dime store. You like it?"

Billy sneezed grandly. "It's strong enough," he said.

"When I buy perfume, I like to get my money's worth."

Snuffling his nose, Billy looked around. "Where's Heather?" Heather was supposed to be a junior this year.

"Home."

"Home for today or home for good?"

"She's sixteen," Gina said, as if that explained everything. "Plus who's going to take care of little Dale shits-his-pants? Not me, that's for sure."

On the highway the school bus picked up speed. Billy didn't join in the usual horseplay. He felt bad about his mother crying. The ride felt long, very long. As he thought about high school—and about Suzy and Kenwood—his stomach bunched up, and he could taste his breakfast sausage higher and higher up in his throat. He let down the window for some air, which mostly cleared his head and settled his stomach.

As the bus arrived at school, Billy squinted through the window. Among the crowd he saw no Suzy, but no gang of town kids waiting for him, either.

"Hey, Billy!" Tiny Tim Loren raced up. "Found your locker yet?"

"I just got off the damn bus."

"We're assigned lockers in alphabetical order," Tim said, leading Billy inside. "So guess who I'm two lockers from?"

"How would I know?"

"Loren, Langen?"

Billy stopped to stare at Tiny Tim.

Tim grinned. "I thought that would get your attention."

Billy shrugged and walked on.

"Trade you lockers?" Tim said.

"Probably not," Billy said.

"Hey, here's your chance with Suzy," Tim added.

"Beat it," Billy said.

"Well, maybe I'll see if King—"

Billy turned and caught Tim by the shirt; he lifted him off the ground and held him at eye level.

"Hey look everybody, I've grown, I'm taller!" Tim called.

Billy lowered him. He didn't want to call attention to himself, not on day one.

"Hey I was just kidding, Billy, kidding," Tiny Tim said as Billy walked away. He caught up with Billy. "Where's the old Billy Baggs sense of humor?"

Billy headed off left, then right down this strange section of the school. His old junior high building, connected by a tunnel, felt far away. Here the boys were as tall as him or taller, and the girls all looked fresh out of the Sears catalogue. Holding his slip of paper with his locker number and combination, keeping his head down, he passed by cliques of juniors and seniors. There was a great divide in the halls. One group was town kids. They talked loudly, easily, and they all seemed to know each other. The other group was shabby, farm and reservation types, as skittish as wild ponies passing down unfamiliar canyons. Billy kept moving.

Finally he found his locker. It was, of course, between two girls, one overweight, one skinny, both pimply, who had already opened theirs and decorated them inside with colored stickers and posters. They giggled as Billy stepped up to his lock, glanced at the combination written in ballpoint ink on his palm, and spun the combination to his locker.

Which of course didn't open.

He kept trying the combination and jerking at the latch.

"Um," ventured the fat girl, "I think you have to turn it right, left *twice* and then right."

Billy tried that and the latch opened. "Thanks," he mumbled.

The girls giggled. Billy checked his watch: only eight periods to go.

His schedule was Basic Science, Social Studies, Introduction to Algebra, gym, lunch, study hall, Shop and English. As the first bell rang, he wondered which classes he would have with Suzy, which with King, which with both.

Neither Suzy nor King were in Basic Science, a class mainly of wild horses. By way of greeting, Shawn Howenstein gave Billy a friendly middle finger, Owen McGinty faked his middle finger up his nose, and Butch Redbird gave a black power salute. Billy nodded, then scanned the room; it was like his crowd was in a whole different school than the college prep types. But Mr. Grundhof, the science teacher, diverted Billy's attention.

A bushy-haired man in glasses and white lab coat, he started class by pouring some kind of liquid into a shallow glass bowl, then turning to write things on the blackboard. The class took the opportunity to goof off and whack each other—until the liquid in the bowl ignited with a loud *SWOOSH!* A ball of flame punched upward, girls screamed, and the boys' mouths fell open with admiration. Mr. Grundhof whirled to face the class. "A form of spontaneous combustion," he announced. "Who in this class knows what spontaneous combustion is?"

The class was silent.

Billy knew exactly what spontaneous combustion was. They had to watch out for it on the farm, particularly in the hayloft. When there was too much moisture in the bales, their own compression and the great weight of other bales on top combined to form heat. Let go long enough, bales would actually begin to smolder, then eventually burst into flames. But Billy wasn't about to raise his hand—certainly not on day one of high school.

Between classes he looked for Suzy, with no luck.

And no luck, either, in Social Studies. Mr. Schlafen, a stooped, balding man, assigned seats, then ran a grainy filmstrip called "The American Experiment in Democracy." There was a scratchy record for the sound track, with a beep to signal a change of filmstrip image. Mr. Schlafen, appearing to nod off briefly, got one beep behind and never caught up.

Between second and third periods Billy scanned the hall for Suzy. No luck.

Algebra was worse yet. The teacher, Mrs. Albani, seemed nice enough, but she went on a twenty-minute ramble about the "value of X." Tiny Tim finally raised his hand.

"Yes?" Mrs. Albani said, happy to have some response.

"Would this X be the same as an X-rated movie?"

Mrs. Albani stared.

"And if so, what is the value of a triple-X-rated movie?" He looked around and yukked it up.

"Mr. Halgrimson's office. Right now," the teacher said, reddening in the face and hoisting Tim along toward the door.

In gym class Billy had to go outside and play kickball in his street clothes. Like most everyone, he had not thought of bringing gym clothes. After forty minutes of racing about, his feet hurt like hell in his cowboy boots, and he was sweaty and hungry and ready for lunch. He was so hungry, he forgot about Suzy.

Which was when he ran into her.

He was carrying his tray of Spanish rice and beans, bread, fruit cup and milk through the cafeteria, when suddenly there she was. They almost banged trays. His heart lurched like some great engine turning over. "Suzy!"

"Billy!" Her eyes widened.

Doug Nixon was just behind Suzy. "Wow!" he

said. "You must get good radio reception with those teeth."

There was laughter. Billy blinked and clamped his mouth shut. For the first time he took in the rest. It was Kenwood and the college-bound crowd. King looked away. Billy set his jaw and moved on with his tray.

"Directly from Kansas, the Tin Man!" someone called after Billy. He spun around, looked for the nearest place to dump his tray in order to free up his fists.

"Hey, Billy!" a voice called. "Let it slide." Butch Redbird appeared from nowhere, gripped Billy's arm and steered him toward a table of farm and reservation kids. "For a second I thought you were going to charge the mound," Butch said, glancing over to the table of town kids.

"I thought about it," Billy muttered as he sat down.

"Man, you got to learn to lighten up, Billy. You got to learn to turn sideways and let bullshit flow on by," Butch said. "Otherwise, you'll always get a faceful, and what fun is that?"

"Who made you the great philosopher?"

"I did," Butch said. "Indians gotta be philosophical. That's all we got left. We lost everything else to you guys."

Billy gave him an annoyed look, then turned to eat.

"By the way, saving your ass will cost you that bread," Butch said, reaching toward Billy's tray.

"It was their asses you saved," Billy retorted, snatching his slice to safety.

"I heard that you almost broke King's arm," Tim said.

"You should, next time," one of the farm kids said.

Billy ignored them. While he ate, he wondered if Suzy would come over and at least say hello. But she never did. And he was weirdly relieved.

In study hall he propped up a book, then leaned his head in his hands. Within seconds he slid down a long slope into sleep. His dream was of dueling King on horseback with lances that were really oversized baseball bats; Suzy Langen was there in a cheerleader's outfit and a tall, princess-type hat, and she cheered them on as they lunged again and again toward each other.

"Hey, Billy!"

He started awake.

"You're mumblin', man. You having a wet dream or what?" Jake the Fake whispered.

Several people in the desks around him giggled. Billy quickly wiped the drool from his wrist and shook his head to clear it.

In shop class, amid the smells of wood and of welding, amid the dull gleam and curve of hand tools and power grinders, amid the familiar saws and lathes, Billy felt at home. Mr. Lengel, the teacher, got their attention by holding up his right hand.

"See this hand?" he said.

They stared. It was missing fingers. The digits, beginning with the pinky and ending with middle one, were gone at a straight, rising angle. "It happened right there, on that table saw." The class looked at the full pointer finger of his other hand. "I was in here after hours, tired, hurrying to finish up a project, my head up my butt, and a second later my fingers—one, two, three—were flying across the room." He swung his hand suddenly to the left; Billy swore he saw the fingers, or at least their ghosts, still in the air, headed toward the sawdust bin. "I had to go find them," Mr. Lengel said, lowering his voice for effect. "I put them in a plastic Baggie and drove to the hospital, but there was nothing the doctor could do."

The class was as quiet as a funeral home.

"My point? In shop class you never, ever hurry or otherwise have your head up your butt."

There was a small, relieved ripple of laughter.

"His hand ain't nothing like a corn picker hand," Billy murmured to Shawn Howenstein.

"Or a sausage grinder hand," Shawn added.

"You two have something to say?" Mr. Lengel said immediately.

"No, sir," Billy and Shawn said quickly together.

"I do," Tiny Tim said waving his hand.

"Yes?"

"So what did they do with your fingers?"

There was laughter.

Mr. Lengel waited his turn. "When I was leaving the hospital, I saw Mrs. Jorgenson carrying a small package. As you know, Mrs. Jorgenson works in the school cafeteria."

The class fell silent.

"The school lunch that day was hot dogs," Mr. Lengel finished.

The class groaned and laughed, and Mr. Lengel went on to outline the projects they would do this semester. In metalworking, students could decide between a handy worm can with soldered belt loops and a side door for easy worm access, or else a sheet metal lockbox with a padlock clasp.

"Either would be very useful for our career developments," whispered Tiny Tim.

Mr. Lengel closed the introductory class by forcing each student to shake hands with him on the way out. The teacher's pink stub fingers felt hard on top and were very smooth.

English class was last. Billy had never enjoyed reading, mainly because it always took him longer than everybody else. He slouched into class, looking for a seat far back, and froze. Right in the middle, already seated, was Suzy. And just ahead of her, King Kenwood. This class was an equal mix of town and country kids. Quickly Billy found a desk in the back row. The teacher, Miss Henderson, was a short, thin woman with salt-and-pepper hair pulled up in back and a dress with a high collar. When the students were all seated, she drew herself up and held up a hand for silence. "Class, welcome to the world of *words*." Billy sighed, and there were faint groans here and there. Suzy Langen frowned at the rudeness.

"One of main readings for this year will be a classic work of drama, *Romeo and Juliet*, which I know you'll enjoy."

There were louder groans, mainly from the boys.

"But, first things first, the seating chart," Miss Henderson, said, taking out her grade book and a class list. "You all have seats; now we're going to find your rightful ones. Alphabetically, starting with desk number one, row one: Abbott, Barry.

"Allen, Sheila."

Students shuffled resignedly forward. Luckily Miss Henderson's chart was arranged up and back rather than sideways; otherwise he'd be stuck in the front row for sure.

"Amundson, Kenneth."

Billy tensed.

"Baggs, William," Miss Henderson announced in her crisp, sharp-edged syllables. Suzy and King both turned to look. Billy glanced briefly their way and trudged to take his seat only four desks back from the front. The displaced students clustered at the rear, and the seating continued up and down the rows. It was just Billy's luck—whether good or bad luck, he was not sure—that Suzy ended up right across from him and one desk forward. At least she was not right beside him. Billy made sure not to look at her. At least for the first five minutes of the class.

After that his eyes never left Suzy. He did not remember hearing another word Miss Henderson said that hour, and the sudden ringing of the bell startled him. As the students rushed toward the door, Billy tried to avoid Suzy, but she cut off his path. Kenwood, with a suspicious look at both of them, reluctantly trailed through the door. Miss Henderson was occupied by a couple of brown-nosers, and suddenly it was just Billy and Suzy.

"Billy," she said quickly, "I'm sorry about this noon. In the cafeteria."

"Sorry for what?"

"For my friends. How they acted."

Billy shrugged. "I don't need them; I got my own friends," he said, setting his jaw. He looked past her, toward the door.

"It's like you're avoiding me," she said. "Why?"

He shrugged again.

"Maybe we should talk about what happened at your farm." She blushed. "I'm sorry—"

"Sorry about the fight?" Billy interrupted. "Or sorry about us?"

She stared, then looked down. "No. I still want to see you sometime. Probably just to talk. You know. . . ."

"If you want to see me, come sit with me. At my table. With my friends."

"Billy, why are you doing this?"

"Hey, Langen, let's go," called a voice from the hallway. King Kenwood stepped back into the doorway. He met Billy's stare. "Unless I'm interrupting something."

"No. We were just talking," Suzy said quickly. "About . . . English class."

There was silence; in the hall, locker doors

slammed with dull thuds. On the wall the big clock ticked.

"Well, are you coming or not?" King said to her. "The gang is headed uptown."

"She can't, and neither can you," Billy said. "You're coming with me, remember?"

King's shoulders slumped an inch. "This has to be a bad dream."

"I wish," Billy added angrily.

Suzy frowned. Puzzled, she looked at them both. "What's going on here?"

"Ask Coach Anderson," the boys said in unison, and turned to the hall and their lockers.

King Kenwood's appearance on Billy's school bus brought absolute silence among the rowdy passengers.

"Got a permission slip?" Bib O'Brien asked.

Sullenly, King withdrew a letter from his overnight bag.

The driver made a show of opening the envelope, of unfolding the page, of getting it right side up. "'I hereby give *reluctant* permission to my son, Archer Kenwood,'" he read loudly, "'to ride on the *appropriate* school bus with Billy Baggs for the next two school days. Signed, Mark Kenwood, *attorney-at-law.*'" Bib grinned, gap-toothed, at King. "Well congratulations, kid. This is the *appropriate* bus."

"Come on," Billy said to King, and led him toward the rear of the bus.

Gaze welded to Billy's back, King followed. Heads turned and voices murmured as he passed.

Billy paused midway down the aisle. "Is there some problem?"

The farm and reservation kids glanced wide-eyed at each other. No one said anything.

"Good. Thank you very much," Billy said, still glaring. Hoisting a sixth-grader from his seat, dropping him across the aisle, Billy nodded at the vacant space. "Sit here," he said. King took the window seat.

The bus lurched forward and began to head out of town. King's head turned as if he was seeing Main Street for the last time. Inside the bus all eyes remained on Billy and King.

"This was not my idea," Billy announced to no one in particular.

"Mine either," muttered King.

Gina Erickson broke the silence. "So what the hell is going on?"

Billy and King glanced briefly at each other, then King looked out at the passing fields.

"Coach Anderson says that if we want to be on the baseball team, we have to spend a whole school week together," Billy muttered.

"Together together?" Gina's eyes dropped to King's overnight bag.

Billy nodded. "He has to live on the farm for half the week, then I gotta go live in town with him for the other half."

There was sudden murmuring and low whistling. "Cruel and unusual," Gina remarked.

"I agree," King grumbled, keeping his eyes

fixed on the landscape outside. As the other passengers gradually returned to their usual knucklehead, hair-pulling behavior, King glanced about cautiously.

"Don't worry, they won't hurt you," Billy said.

"I can take care of myself," King said. "Though for the next three days that's your job, isn't it?"

Billy didn't bother with a reply.

They rode along in silence. The bus turned off the blacktop and onto washboarded gravel.

"How long does the ride take?" King asked.

"An hour," Billy said.

"An hour?" King replied, looking at Billy fully for the first time. "You mean, like a half hour each way?"

Billy shook his head. "Hour in the morning, hour at night."

King considered this. "So what time do you get on the bus in the morning?"

"A few minutes before seven."

"Good grief," King muttered, and turned back to his window.

Abner was at the farm driveway to greet the bus. "Welcome to the real world, kid," he said to Kenwood. He tossed him a new pair of work gloves. King caught the gloves and stared at them. Then he looked over his shoulder at the school bus disappearing in a cloud of dust.

In the kitchen Mavis, home early to make sure everything went all right on King's first day, worked amid the smell of fresh cinnamon rolls and hot chocolate.

"Welcome to our house, Archer," she said.

King nodded warily. "Thank you," he murmured. He looked around, his eyes taking in the wood-burning stove, the linoleum floor, the old refrigerator and range.

"I suppose this don't look like much compared to your house," Abner said.

"None of that," Mavis said sharply to her husband. "Billy, take Archer's bag to your room."

"My room?" He lowered his voice. "My room? I thought he was staying in the spare room."

"Your room. You and him have to be together, remember? That was the agreement."

Billy rolled his eyes and jerked his head for King to follow him up the narrow stairway.

"Watch—" Billy began.

There was a sharp thud as King whacked his forehead on the low ceiling beam.

"—your head," Billy finished.

King blinked, rubbed his skull, then trudged after Billy. They passed down the short hall, Billy pausing by a closed door. "This room was my brother's room. Nobody goes in there, particularly you." Billy moved on to the end of the hall and his own little door. "This is my room. I take the bed; you've got the roll-away." The two of them barely fit into the narrow room with the sharply sloped roof.

King looked around. "Is there a bathroom?"

"Where? Here?"

"Anywhere. In the house, I mean."

"No," Billy said, "we shit in the woods and take our showers when it rains."

King stared cautiously at him.

"Of course there's a damn bathroom. It's downstairs, off the kitchen."

King looked relieved.

"So now you've seen where you sleep. Let's go eat, 'cause I've—we've—got chores to do."

At the kitchen table Abner was waiting, leaned back in his chair, nursing a cup of coffee. He was in the most pleasant of moods. "It's gonna be nice to have a free hired hand around here for a few days," he said. "I might just sleep in tomorrow morning. Even take me a vacation, like people in town do."

"Abner . . ." Mavis began.

"A paid vacation, that would be even better."

"Haven't you got something to do?" Mavis asked. "Outside?"

"Nope, not me anyway," Abner said. He kept smiling at King, who took a chair at maximum distance.

They chewed and sipped and swallowed in silence. Abner kept his nonstop gaze on King.

King cleared his throat. "These are excellent cinnamon rolls," he murmured.

"Why, thank you," Mavis said. She glanced at Billy and Abner. "No one's told me that for a long time."

"Some of the best I've ever eaten," King added.

Billy rolled his eyes.

"Well, eat up," Abner said to King. "Takes a lot of calories for farm work."

King, glancing at the kitchen clock, appeared to chew slightly slower, as if this was his last meal.

In the mud porch King pulled on coveralls that Mavis had set out. They were clean, ironed, and worn soft, with one purple patch at the left knee. Billy flinched as he saw the purple patch; he stalked back into the kitchen and whispered hoarsely to his mother. "Why is he wearing those? Those were Robert's!"

"I didn't think it would hurt," she murmured. "They really were hand-me-downs from your father."

"To Robert," Billy said. He glared at King, who stood looking confused.

"Well, it's too late now," Mavis said firmly, setting out Robert's manure boots as well. "And besides, I don't see why we shouldn't get some use from them."

Billy blew out a breath and brushed past King. "Let's go," he said, and headed outside.

King pulled on the boots and clumped after Billy.

"That's the machine shed. The granary. The chicken coop. The well house," Billy said, jerking his head this way and that.

"What's a well house?"

Billy glanced at King. "A well? As in a pipe that goes down into the ground and brings up water?"

King shrugged. "I thought you meant 'well,' as in you sit there and get well, or something."

Billy could only shake his head.

"So I'm allowed to ask, right?" King said sharply.

They walked on in silence.

Near the barn Abner was waiting with the little tractor hooked to the manure spreader. "I thought we'd muck out that south calf pen," he called. "It's been a while."

"Great," Billy said. "I knew he'd pull something like this."

"Like what?" King said.

"You don't want to know."

Inside the barn King paused to wrinkle his nose, to let his eyes adjust. Billy looked around, seeing the barn through a stranger's eyes: the dim yellow necklace of lightbulbs stretching along the feed alley; the low ceilings, the massive beams that held up the hayloft just above them; the old wooden stanchions to the right; the calf pens to the left; the battered whitewashed walls all around. This was an old-time barn, built for fork and shovel. No fancy equipment for Abner Baggs (and no fancy bank payment, either, he would be quick to add).

"The dairy barn," Billy announced, holding his arms wide. "We milk the cows over here, and the milk house is through that swinging door."

"Where are the cows?"

"In the pasture. They'll be here soon enough."

King nodded.

"My usual afternoon routine is to clean the gutter, scrape the platform and put some fresh straw down," Billy said. "That way it's nice and clean for milking. After that I feed silage and grain, then let the cows into the barn."

"The gutter looks empty."

"Lucky for us my old man cleaned it this morning," Billy said. "He wants us to do the calf pen instead."

King looked to the side; several black-and-white calves, alerted by their voices, bounded and thudded loudly against the sides of the pen, which was about twelve feet square.

"What about the calves?" King said. "Will they stay in there when we clean it?"

"Sure, why not?" Billy said.

Outside the barn, and past the open top half of the Dutch door, came the rattle of the tractor, and Abner. "Howdy, boys," he said, leaning down to salute them as he went by. Behind him came the empty manure spreader, which halted before the doorway.

"Now what?" King said.

"From here on it's fairly simple," Billy said, and handed him a fork.

King, holding its tines out like a weapon, eased behind Billy into the pen.

"They won't hurt you," Billy said, giving the closest calf a sharp rap on the skull with his wooden fork handle. The calf staggered, blinked and for a second widened the stance of its four hooves.

"Beat it! Go away!" King said, fending off a smaller one.

"They're just hungry. Soon as we're done, we'll feed them." And with that Billy set to work.

King, trying to keep one hand over his nose, the calves away with a foot, pitched one forkful to Billy's three. Billy had supposed it would be this way.

"Keep it coming, boys; we don't have all afternoon," Abner called.

After a while Billy stopped and looked about, sniffing. "What's that smell?"

King looked at him like he was insane.

Billy poked his head out the door, and saw his father perched on the tractor seat, hands behind his head and smoking a small Tiparillo cigar. Muttering, Billy returned to his work.

After fifteen minutes on the top layer of bedding, which was mostly straw and dried manure, they reached the middle layer, which was heavier and wetter and stronger smelling.

"Damn," King said, wiping his eyes.

"Gets riper the deeper you go," Billy said.

King's face was very white. Trying to breathe into his collar, he kept struggling with forkfuls of the piss-soaked bedding. From outside came the sound of Abner Baggs whistling a tuneless song and the rank smell of his cigar. They worked on, down to the concrete, where the straw was hot and wet and carried the nose-biting odor of ammonia. Suddenly, with a great *"Errrrrp,"* King bent over and sprayed chocolate and cinnamon-roll chunks.

Billy leaped sideways to avoid the blast.

"Sorry," King muttered, hands on his knees. Work stopped as King spit and hawked to clear his mouth.

"Any problems, boys?" Abner said, poking his head into the doorway.

"No—we're fine," Billy said.

"Just fine," King said quickly. Spitting one last time, he attacked the last corner of the pen. Abner ducked out of sight as dripping forkfuls began to fly in faster and faster rhythm.

"Now we're talking," called Abner from outside. "That'll build strength in your pitching arms."

King swore to himself and kept working. Within minutes his fork tines sparked on concrete.

"Good enough; we ain't cleaning a church!" Billy said. He, too, was panting.

King leaned against the pen wall and wiped his face. His coveralls were spattered to the knees with dung, and black at the armpits and chest from sweat. Calves nuzzled and butted his legs and hands.

"Take a break," Billy said, pointing beyond the pen. He was sweating, and happy to stop. "I'll get some fresh straw."

Outside, Abner brought up the rpms and headed off to the field. King went to the milk house to wash his face.

When Billy returned from the hayloft, carrying a bale of straw in each hand, King was waiting, gloves on. "What's next?"

Billy tossed the fresh yellow bales into the pen. "Break the twine and kick the straw around."

King set to work. Soon the calves were bounding and frolicking upon their fresh bedding, until one stopped to take a long, frothy piss, and a fat brown dump for good measure. King stared.

"They'll do it every time," Billy observed.

After finishing the calf pen, King followed Billy into the silo room. "Now we have to go up and throw down silage."

In the small lean-to space that connected barn to silo, King peered up the chute. "We climb up there?" he asked.

"Afraid of heights?"

"I've climbed the water tower in town," King said, shrugging. "It's a lot higher than this silo."

"Good. But wait until I get back," Billy said. "We've got to air out the silo before we go up." He went to get the silage cart, which was at the far end of the feed alley, then looked around for a second fork.

When he returned, King was nowhere to be seen. Puzzled, Billy looked around; he'd been gone only a couple of minutes. Then he heard a faint, rhythmic scraping sound far above him in the silo's chute. He leaned forward and peered upward. High up in the chute, King's boots twitched against tin, jerking spasmodically; his head and shoulders were out of sight, slumped inside the silo.

"No, King!" Billy shouted. "Silo gas!"

Billy hauled himself up, scrambling, grabbing, bounding up the iron rungs. At the top he grabbed King's legs. With a terrific jerk he wrenched him free. King was limp and heavy and silent. His eyeballs were rolled back; only the whites showed. Billy hoisted King across his shoulders and manhandled him, bouncing and jerking, down the chute. King began to cough.

"Hang on," Billy shouted, as they crashed the last few feet to the floor. Dragging King like a sack of oats, Billy got him outside into the fresh air.

"Wake up, come on!" Billy shouted, slapping him again and again, openhanded, across the face.

Suddenly King held up his hands protectively. "Cut it out! Cut it out!"

"You stupid fool!" Billy yelled. He balled a fist, felt like punching him.

"Whaa happened?" King said. He blinked in the sunlight.

"Silo gas, you idiot!"

King looked at him blankly.

"I told you to wait up, that we had to air out the silo!"

King stared. "I figured the silo couldn't smell any worse than that calf pen."

Billy let out a breath and rolled onto his side on the ground. His voice shook. "Silo gas you don't smell. Another minute and you'd have been dead."

King's eyes widened.

Billy helped him into the milk house, where King ran water over his head and mopped his face with cold towels. When he was done, Billy had a milking stool waiting for him.

"Sit," he commanded.

King, coughing one last time, shaking his head to clear away the cobwebs, obeyed.

"The deal is, there are a dozen ways you can get killed on the farm," Billy said. "Believe me, I know this to be true." For a moment his voice faltered. "Anyway, since I'm supposed to be looking out for you this week, you'd better learn what they are."

King gave Billy his full attention as they toured the farm. Their first stop was the tractor and hump-shaped silage blower stationed at the base of the silo. "Power takeoffs, for example," Billy explained. He pointed to the stubby axle, long as a broomstick and twice as thick, that connected the rear of the tractor to the base of the silage blower. "A power takeoff transfers power from the tractor's engine to an implement, like this blower, or a hay mower, or a baler. It spins just like an axle on a car."

King nodded.

"The thing is, axles on cars are protected and out of sight. Power takeoffs sometimes aren't covered, and they're always right up where you could trip and get wound up in them," Billy continued.

He started up the tractor engine. King flinched slightly at the noise, then watched the shaft begin to turn. "This one has a protective outer sleeve that doesn't turn," Billy called, "which is no guarantee of anything. Sometimes the sleeve gets rusted to the shaft, and they both turn. I knew this guy who tried to step over a power takeoff but slipped down onto it. The power takeoff ripped out his crotch."

"Of his pants?" King said.

"No, his real crotch," Billy said.

King leaned away slightly.

"Whacked off everything," Billy added. "Scooped him clean." It was a true story.

King's eyes widened. "Did he . . . die?"

"Not right away," Billy said. "After he got out of the hospital and healed up, he started to drink. Heavy boozing. Everybody knew what had happened to him, right? Particularly his wife, if you get what I mean. Eventually she left him, and a year or two later he went into his machine shed and blew his brains out with a shotgun."

King swallowed. Billy brought up the rpms and let the blower whine full speed. When bits of chaff and kernels of corn wafted down from the silo, Billy powered down the engine.

"Aired out. Now we can go up there safely," he said.

King stared at the tall silo.

"If you're still game," Billy added.

"After you."

While they pitched silage down the chute, Billy lectured King on the other dangers of farm life, from electrical cords falling into water tanks to being crushed by Holstein bulls. When he finished, King said, "That's only eight."

"Eight?"

"You said there were a dozen ways to get killed on the farm."

"Oh there are way more than a dozen," Billy said. "Trouble is, I don't know what they are."

King leaned on his fork as he thought about that.

Feeding and milking the cows proceeded without a hitch. King, with newfound caution, made sure to stay back two paces from Fussy, a Holstein whose greatest pleasure in life was to whack a man's shin (or better, his forehead) with her right hind hoof. Billy also saved him from Dipshit, who found bovine fulfillment by dragging the fluffy switch of her tail in the gutter, then whipping it across the milker's face. By six-thirty P.M. they were done with chores and headed up to the house for supper.

King was stumbling tired. "You do this every night?"

"And morning," Billy said.

"Great," King muttered.

At the supper table, after Mavis said the blessing,

she paused to look at King. "Are you feeling all right?" she asked.

"I'm fine," King said, glancing at Billy. "Just a little hungry, I guess."

"Real work will do that to you," Abner remarked.

King ate more Swiss steak, carrots and spuds than Billy had seen since Big Danny Boyer last bellied up to this table. Mavis kept the bowls moving, Abner the conversation.

"So, there, Mr. Kenwood, what do you think of farm life so far?"

"He's only been here a few hours," Billy said.

"Well, most people never spend one hour of their lives on a farm, let alone get to clean a calf pen," Abner said.

"You didn't!" Mavis said to Abner. She turned to stare at him.

Abner shrugged. "From all that Farm Team baseball, more than a few chores have been let slide around here."

"Well, just so Archer knows we don't clean calf pens every day," Mavis added.

"That's a small relief," King said.

"Think of it as your contribution to playing baseball on our field," Abner said.

"Pa!" Billy said.

"Fair enough," King replied.

"How about some apple pie?" Mavis said quickly.

King stood up and began to take his plate to the sink. Abner and Billy stared at him. "What is it

156

you're doing?" Abner said. King paused, gravy-smeared plate in hand; he looked about.

"I'll tell you what he's doing," Mavis said. "He's clearing his own dishes. He obviously has been brought up to help out around the house. Not like some people I know."

Billy sank lower in his chair.

"Just keep going, Archer," Mavis said, pointing him toward the sink. "Billy, you too. And on your way, take your father's plate."

Billy cast a dark look at King, then obeyed.

"In fact," Mavis said, "from this night forward that's how it's going to be around this house. Either clear your own dishes or you don't get dessert."

With Abner glowering at him, King looked more frightened than when he had survived silo gas. To avoid Abner, King stayed with Mavis in the kitchen after supper.

"It's very nice of you to help with the dishes," Mavis said.

"No problem," King said.

Abner, listening to Twins baseball on the radio, glanced toward the kitchen. "Clearing the table. Wiping dishes. This could be a mistake," he said.

"No kidding," Billy replied.

Much later that night, Billy lay in silence in his dusky room. King lay equally quiet, an arm's length away.

After a long while King said, "By the way, thanks for . . . this afternoon. You know."

"For saving your ass?" Billy said.

King shrugged. In the shadows he nodded.

"Forget about it," Billy said. "Anybody would have done the same thing."

King had no reply.

The next morning, after chores, showers and a pancake breakfast, King and Billy waited for the school bus. King kept squinting down the road as if the bus was his ticket back to civilization.

"Don't worry, it's coming," Billy said.

Soon a rumbling flower of dust grew, brown at the edges, orange at its center. Gears groaned, brakes squealed and a breath of exhaust and dust washed over them. King followed Billy up the steps. Bib O'Brien leaned over to sniff King as he passed. "What *is* that smell?"

King quickly looked down at his clothes. Bib laughed.

"That smell is you," Billy said to the driver, and jerked his head for King to move along.

"Watch your mouth, Billy-boy," Bib warned, "or you'll be walking to school."

"Someday it's gonna be payback time for that loser," Billy said.

"Count me in," King said.

"So, are you two best friends now or what?" Gina Erickson said brightly. She was sitting across from them. Snapping her gum behind bright-red lipstick, Gina was wearing a tight, low-cut black top and golden hoop earrings as large as coffee cups. Her outfit guaranteed two pink slips from the principal (yesterday her high heels had gotten her the first). King, intending to give Gina a brief and annoyed glance, let his eyes slip to her chest.

"It's a push-up bra," Billy said.

"It ain't either," Gina said instantly.

"How would King know?" Billy teased.

Gina looked quickly about the bus to see if Bib O'Brien was watching; around her there were encouraging whoops and yips. She began to peel down the shoulders of her top.

"Gina, I was just kidding," Billy said quickly.

"Well, I'm not," she said.

"I believe you, I believe you!" King said.

"Are you sure?" Gina said, standing.

King swallowed. "Nearly positive."

"*Nearly* positive?" Her hands went back to her shoulder straps.

"Positive! Definitely!" King said.

Gina giggled and settled back. "Anyway, Billy knows for sure. Right, Billy?"

Billy looked out his window. Since he didn't deny this, whoops and hoots and cackles flooded his way. Soon the bus was its usual raucous, rolling nuthouse on wheels.

"Is it always like this?" King said.

"Pretty much," Billy said. "One time, when Big Danny Boyer was still going to school . . ." He began to tell King about the time some older boys talked Danny entirely out of his clothes, then threw them out the window, and what happened when Danny arrived at school. Halfway into the story, Billy looked over at his seatmate. King was silent. Slumped against the glass, his face mashed into the window, he was sound asleep.

Billy let him doze. He usually slid into a trance himself about now. The bus turned onto the highway and picked up speed. Gina rhythmically popped her gum, and the telephone poles slung themselves past. Billy leaned back and stared vacantly at the fields and groves.

When he blinked again, the bus was slowing for the Flint city limits. King was tipped over sideways in the seat, out of sight, snoring quietly.

Gina, her perfume overpowering, leaned close and nudged Billy. "I told everybody to be real quiet," she whispered. "We'll all get off, and leave your pal King here. He'll probably sleep all the way to the bus barn. Bib will never notice him."

Billy thought about it. "Naw, we'd better not."

"It'd be a great trick," Gina said.

"I'm supposed to stay with him this week, not give him the slip."

"Some fun you are," Gina said.

The bus braked, and the others eased down the aisle. King stirred but did not wake up.

"Well at least let me wake him up, then," Gina said.

"How?" Billy asked suspiciously. They were nearly last on the bus now.

"Watch this. He'll think he's dreaming."

Billy sighed and stood up. Gina slipped into his seat and crouched low alongside King's face. From behind, Billy saw Gina lower her straps partway and put her cleavage an inch from King's face. "King, dear . . . time to wake up."

King murmured something. Then his eyes opened. "My God!" he said, and sat bolt upright.

"No, but boys seem to like them," Gina said. She laughed and leaned away. "Have a nice day, King. You, too, Billy," she said, as she sashayed down the aisle.

King looked up at Billy, who shrugged. "You were sleeping so hard, I figured it was the only way."

At school Billy was free of King until lunch, when they had to sit together. It was part of the deal, which the whole ninth grade seemed to know about. Eyes averted, carrying his tray, King passed his usual table. "Have fun, King," one of his friends called.

"Keep the conversation going!" said a second.

"If that's possible," added a third. There was laughter from the town crowd. King glared at them. Suzy Langen said nothing. She followed King and Billy with her eyes.

At the far table Butch Redbird said, "So, King, how'd it go last night?"

King shrugged as he plopped down his tray. "Well, I'm still alive."

The farm and reservation kids laughed at the joke. Billy and King glanced briefly at each other and almost smiled.

Billy's friends kept the conversation going during lunch.

"Hey, King, do you have any money on you?" asked Darrel Wind.

"A little; why?" King said cautiously.

"I need to buy a car," Darrel said.

There was choking, eye-watering laughter at the table, enough to draw attention of a cafeteria monitor. King didn't get the joke at all.

Billy was clear of King through the afternoon, until English class. Miss Henderson introduced *Romeo and Juliet* by beginning to read aloud the prologue:

"Two households, both alike in dignity,
In fair Verona, where we lay our scene,
From ancient grudge break to new mutiny . . ."

He sighed. Three lines, and he was drowsy. For him an English class was like a sleeping pill. He vaguely heard Miss Henderson drone on as she summarized the cast of characters and introduced the plot. His eyelids felt like concrete blocks.

"There is, you'll notice, a good deal of fighting in this play," Miss Henderson remarked.

"All right!" Jake Robertson said enthusiastically.

"Swordplay that ends in death and tragedy," Miss Henderson added.

"What can you do?" Jake sighed.

"Perhaps if Tybalt and Mercutio had known each other better, or if Romeo and Tybalt had spent time together, such fighting could have been avoided—would you agree, Mr. Baggs?"

Billy started; he blinked. Miss Henderson was staring straight at him.

"Say no," Jake whispered.

"I would say . . . probably . . . yes," Billy answered.

"I agree, Mr. Baggs," she said, giving him a pointed stare.

After school Abner was waiting at the mailbox in the pickup. Big Danny Boyer sat in the rear. "Welcome home, boys," Abner said cheerfully.

King glanced sideways at Billy; he glanced cautiously at Big Danny, at his matted, greasy hair and his massive arms.

"Don't worry, there ain't any more calf pens to clean," Abner said.

"Well, what then?" Billy said. If Big Danny was here, it meant that Abner was getting up a work crew. Billy hopped into the truck's box and pretended to punch Big Danny in the gut; Big Danny, who was smelling mighty ripe, smiled.

"Nothing real tough," Abner said. "I thought maybe after your snack we would buzz-saw that pile of logs."

Billy sighed.

After sandwiches and chocolate milk Billy and King shrugged on coveralls and boots. Danny wore his usual busted-out tennis shoes and no gloves. The crew headed out to the woodlot.

Stacked back behind the barn near the sawmill was a rick of logs, dullish brown jack pine, of various lengths and diameters. These were not freshly cut saw logs to be milled into lumber and then into finished boards, but downed and dead trees for firewood. The pile was about twenty feet long. Beside it sat a faded orange Allis-Chalmers tractor. A round iron buzz perched on its snout. The saw blade was as wide as a truck tire and had teeth like a dinosaur's. From a distance the little tractor looked like a giant carnivorous insect.

"This won't take but an hour, boys," Abner called as he started up the engine of the little Allis.

"Right," Billy muttered, glancing at the tall pile of logs.

King watched the belt turn, the blade began to spin; within seconds the big iron plate hummed at high rpms. He glanced at the pile of logs.

"You've got it," Billy called above the noise. "I'll take the front of the log, you take the rear. We just keep stepping forward. Danny will throw the blocks off to the side into a pile."

"Ready?" Abner shouted. He remained aboard the tractor to handle the throttle, and to kill the engine if anything went wrong.

Danny positioned himself across the carriage a

long step from the blade; Danny knew buzz saws. Billy cleared the ground where he and King would be stepping, kicking away two limbs and a small round stone. This was not the place to trip and fall.

"Okay," Billy called. He and King seized the first log and advanced it to the blade. With a sound like a giant bumblebee passing at high speed, the blade whined through the log. King's eyes widened. Danny tossed the first round over his shoulder. "About two feet long," Abner shouted.

In short order the first log was reduced to a scattering of round stubs. And so they continued, log by log. Big Danny stood focused and impassive, flipping the rounds over his shoulder as if they were toy building blocks. Abner remained on the tractor, watching. This annoyed Billy greatly. There was no reason why Abner couldn't go and be useful somewhere else.

The crew pressed on. It was a warm Indian summer afternoon.

"*Eyow!*" sang the saw blade.

"*Clunkety, clunk,*" went the block onto the pile.

After fifteen minutes stinging sweat began to leak into Billy's eyes. He swiped at his face with a sleeve between logs, but there was hardly time. King always had the next log hoisted and ready. At the twenty-minute mark Billy held up a hand and stepped backward; Abner ratcheted down the rpms to idle speed.

"Something the matter?" Abner called.

"I thought King might need a break," Billy said.

"Whenever," King said. He was hardly sweating. Big Danny, who never sweated, had no comment.

They all took a drink of water from the jug; then Abner again brought up the rpms. The biggest logs were deeper in the pile, and after another twenty minutes Billy's arms felt heavier than wet wood. King and Big Danny did not seem tired at all. Billy could throw smaller weights, hay bales and shovels full of grain, all day long, but dead weight was not his strong suit.

On the next large log he struggled briefly getting his end off the ground.

"Want me to get it?" King called.

Billy shook his head quickly and waved King away. He felt Abner's eyes on him.

They continued. Beneath the whirring blade grew a cone of sawdust, dusty yellow, crawling with black ants and pine beetles. The afternoon sunlight angled lower and lower, beginning to glare. Small rivers of sweat now ran into Billy's eyes. They stung, obscuring his vision, but he kept on. He kept on because he could feel his father's eyes. King was an unstoppable robot. Billy's arms began to tremble. He should have called for a break—his arms had nothing left—they felt like he had pitched thirty innings in a row. He should have called a halt, but he didn't.

And then it happened.

Struggling with a massive horn-limbed log, hoisting it toward the saw, Billy lost his grip. The log slipped toward his waist, and as he grabbed for it, his sleeve caught on the sharp, trimmed end of a limb. King, at the other end of the log, perhaps in the trance that comes from repetitive work, kept advancing toward the blade. For Billy, time shifted to slow motion. As he lost his balance, as he felt himself falling very slowly, he saw the great iron wheel reaching out to greet his arm. He saw with odd, nearly microscopic clarity the shiny, black half body of a carpenter ant struggling in the sawdust.

"Watch out!" Abner shouted.

And at the last second Billy was wrenched backward.

King.

King had felt the log slip, felt the shift in weight or angle, or perhaps heard Abner. When he looked up, he saw Billy falling. With a lunging jerk he yanked the log sideways, and Billy with it. Billy tumbled to the ground as the blade hissed along his side.

Abner jerked back the rpms. "Billy!" he shouted as he scrambled from the tractor.

Billy looked down at himself, at his left sleeve. The fabric from his elbow to his wrist hung open and tattered, its edges wispy with severed threads. Big Danny stared; he looked down at his own arm.

"Jesus, are you all right?" Abner said. His face, white and drawn, was suddenly close overhead.

"I'm fine," Billy said. He stood up. He was suddenly and intensely angry, though at what he wasn't certain. "Let's go. Let's get back to work. We've got to finish the pile."

Abner looked at King, then Billy. "I think we've done enough today."

King was silent. Billy walked away. Behind, the bright buzz-saw blade spun on and on, turning by its own mindless weight.

"Jesus, that blade would have cut your arm off," King breathed, catching up to him. His face was white.

"But it didn't, did it?" Billy said.

During milking, when King was out of earshot, Abner cleared his throat and turned to Billy. "Out there at the sawmill, I didn't mean to push you boys," he began.

Billy had no comment.

"I don't know what I was thinking."

"I do," Billy said.

Abner looked sideways at Billy.

"You were trying to show King that I was a better man than him."

Abner swallowed. "At least show him how real men have to work."

"Well, maybe I'm not a real man yet," Billy said angrily.

He felt Abner's eyes on him. His father's mouth opened, but he could not find the words. Instead, he reached out to touch Billy's tattered sleeve and felt the frayed edge of fabric through which the blade had passed. "That old saw should have a guard. Let's not use it again until I get something welded."

Billy worked on. "Fine by me," he said.

"Also, best not let your mother see that rip," Abner added.

When the boys came in for supper, Mavis quickly spotted Billy's coveralls. "What in the world happened to your sleeves?" she said.

Billy glanced down at his two bare forearms, then at the ragged line of fabric across both biceps. "Too hot today for long sleeves. I cut them off with my jackknife."

"I have scissors and a sewing machine for that kind of thing," she said sharply.

"Sorry, Ma, wasn't thinking," Billy said, glancing at his father.

"I would agree," she answered, greatly annoyed. "Now get along. Supper's ready."

Later that night, in his room, Billy lay in the shadows with his eyes open. He turned over, then over again in his bed.

At length King said, "Go ahead. You can say it."

"Say what?"

"Thanks for saving my ass."

Billy lay there a good long while, then let out an exasperated breath. "Thanks for saving my ass."

"No sweat," King said. "Now we're even."

They lay there. King shifted in his bed. "I never knew farming was so dangerous."

"It's only dangerous when you're tired or stupid," Billy answered. Then he yawned.

They were silent again. Outside, a nighthawk called. Just above their beds the attic, cooling after the day's heat, creaked and ticked like a ship rocking against invisible waves. Billy was just dozing off when King said, "How did it happen?"

"Huh?" Billy said, opening his eyes.

"When your brother died."

Billy closed them again. In this moment just before sleep, when his body felt light, his bed suspended in the dusky light, the whole house adrift high over farm, he spoke.

"Robert was teaching me how to drive the tractor, but I was too young," Billy said. "My foot slipped off the clutch. He fell down between the tractor and the disk. I didn't know how to stop it, so he got run over by the disk."

"Jesus," King murmured.

They were both silent for a while.

"I heard it was your father who was driving," King said.

"He took the blame," Billy replied. "But it was me."

King did not speak for several minutes. If there was one thing Billy could find to like about King, it was this silence, right now.

"It's strange," King said at length. "My brother, he's the big star in my family. All-state baseball player, big thrower at Iowa, now in Triple-A ball. We never got along all that well. We used to fight all the time, and he'd beat the crap out of me. Now, sometimes when he calls after a game and my father hangs on the phone with him, going over every inning, every batter, I wish sometimes I didn't have a brother."

"No you don't," Billy said.

The next morning Abner passed King the plate of bacon. "Well, Archer, this is your last day on the farm."

"I guess so," King said. He looked straight at Abner now; he was not quite so afraid of him now.

"So what's your verdict on farm life?"

King thought for a long moment. "The food is excellent."

Mavis laughed. Even Abner smiled. Abner passed him the pancakes. "You're not the worst hand at work, either," he allowed.

"Coming from you, Mr. Baggs, that's a compliment," King said.

As they finished breakfast, Abner prepared to head outside. "Just don't go and forget right away what farm life is like," he said to King.

"Believe me, I won't," King answered. Then Abner stepped forward and shook hands with King. Billy got an instant lump in his throat.

Down at the mailbox, with the sun low and red,

the two boys waited for the school bus in silence. King looked back at the farm. "Your old man is a piece of work."

"Ain't it the truth," Billy said.

"I thought my father was hard-boiled . . ." King began, but then ran out of words.

"Maybe all fathers are pieces of work," Billy said.

"Could be," King allowed, "but I think you and me got bigger pieces than most."

They stood in silence as a meadowlark called and the red sun struggled up from the east fields.

This morning Billy carried his overnight bag, and it was he who kept staring down the road for the bus. When they boarded, King moved easily down the aisle, slipping a fake blow from Andy Bronczyk, sending a fake jab at Luke Rasmus. Attention focused on Billy's overnight bag.

"City slicker!"

"Easy Street!"

"No shit to shovel tonight!"

Billy ignored the yahoos and took his seat beside King.

"You know, I'm actually going to miss this," King said, looking around the bus. "It's like going to the zoo every day."

Across the aisle, Gina popped her gum loudly.

The schoolday passed far too quickly, except for last-hour English class. Miss Henderson "accidentally" chose Billy and King to read aloud the parts of Tybalt and Benvolio, their argument in scene 1.

Clearly the entire teaching staff knew about the "contract" between Billy and King; it was downright embarrassing. The two got through the scene by reading their lines in absolute monotone voices. People giggled, Miss Henderson frowned and Suzy Langen looked disgusted.

"Let's try that again with another pair of readers, ones with a bit more pizzazz," the teacher said.

"I agree," Billy muttered.

Miss Henderson kept Billy and King after class. "I'm sorry; I shouldn't have done that," she said. "I was rather obvious."

They shrugged. "It's all right, Miss Henderson," King said.

"Everybody knows about us anyway," Billy added.

She raised one eyebrow and surveyed the two boys. "And are you making progress?"

King and Billy looked at each other.

"As long as he doesn't bite his thumb at me," Billy said.

"Or draw his naked weapon at me," King added.

"I'd say. Now run along," Miss Henderson said dryly.

Suzy was waiting in the hall.

Billy and King looked at each other; their good humor faded.

"So. This is your time to stay in town?" Suzy said.

"Through Saturday," Billy said. He hitched up

his bag and followed King. Neither of them knew quite where to walk in relation to Suzy.

"So, King, what's it like on the regular school bus?" Suzy said brightly as she stepped between Billy and him.

"You don't want to know," King said.

The boys walked woodenly beside her.

"So what are you two going to do after school?" she asked.

"Nothing," King said. "Football practice doesn't begin until next week."

"So? You two could practice baseball," Suzy said. "It's what King usually does all evening."

"I didn't bring my glove," Billy said. He sent a dark look to King; the Jim Kaat glove was still missing.

Soon they entered Green Lawn, and Suzy turned up Venus Lane.

"Maybe I'll drop by later," she said cheerfully.

King gave her a small nod and looked down to kick at a pebble. Billy could give her only a pained look. Then he and King walked on, silent, the mood around them chilly.

"Here we are," King soon said, pointing up the sidewalk.

Billy took a deep breath.

The Kenwood front door was made of carved wood, with narrow colored glass panels on each side. On the bright white concrete below were potted rosebushes in front of the glass panels, and a mailbox with a bright brass eagle on it.

"We're home," King called into the house as they stepped inside.

Billy drew up in the cool, dim air.

"She's got the damn air conditioning on Freeze again," King muttered.

"Archer? Is that you, dear?" came his mother's voice. There was a faint clink of glass and the sound of a small door closing. They stepped into the living room, which was pale-carpeted, sunken and nearly as wide as the Baggs house. It reminded Billy of an ice arena. He expected Mrs. Kenwood to come skating toward them.

Instead, she rose from a white leather couch and a scattering of magazines and weaved toward them. King stiffened.

"I thought it was . . . tomorrow night that you'd be home."

"It's obviously today," King said.

"Then this is your new farm friend, Billy Baggs!" She smiled lopsidedly. "I almost didn't recognize you, considering how you looked last time—"

"That's enough, Mother," King said.

Billy, embarrassed, nodded hello. King's mother reached out to shake hands; her fingers were very cold, as if her blood were air-conditioned or she had been holding a glass filled with ice cubes.

"Welcome, welcome, welcome," she went on, continuing to smile at Billy and looking him up and down.

King brushed past her. "Is there anything to eat?"

"There's fruit."

"I want a sandwich."

"King, dear, you never eat sandwiches after school," his mother said.

"I do now," King mumbled, poking his head into the refrigerator. Billy got a flash of its interior; it was mainly white empty racks and shelves.

"I didn't get the grocery shopping done," his mother said. "I'll go now."

"No you won't," King said, approaching his mother. "Make some coffee, and I'll walk down to the market and get something."

"Coffee? Why would I need coffee?" his mother said, her voice whiny.

King turned to glare at her.

"I'd have a cup," Billy said. "Once in a while I drink coffee." Billy didn't meet King's eyes: He would not wish this scene on his worst enemy.

"Well sure, then, I'll make coffee," Mrs. Kenwood said, her lopsided smile returning. "Why didn't you say so?"

"Is there some grocery money?" King said.

"In the cupboard, dear."

King reached in for a glass jar; it was filled with green bills, a roll of tens and twenties. He peeled off several.

"For dinner, get . . . whatever," Mrs. Kenwood said.

Billy moved to follow King. "Archer will be right back," Mrs. Kenwood said, putting a hand on his arm. "You stay, and I'll show you around, get you situated. All right, Archer dear?"

King paused. He looked questioningly at Billy, who nodded. "Have your coffee first. I'll be right back," King said to his mother, then the door slammed shut after him.

"Sit. Relax," Mrs. Kenwood gestured grandly to Billy.

Billy perched on the edge of a high kitchen stool. He looked around. Large copper pots, with no sign of use, hung down from a polished wooden rack. Bright white tile embossed with pale seashell figures ran behind the white sink and white range. Billy could see no food anywhere. He imagined there must be, somewhere, a pantry, somewhere a freezer full of meat.

Mrs. Kenwood fumbled with a small container, spilling several coffee beans; they skittered across the floor; Billy hurried to retrieve them. "That's terribly kind of you," Mrs. Kenwood said. "Just toss them in the trash." Then a sudden sharp grinding noise startled Billy.

"Fresh-ground coffee," she said. "It's what I cook best."

Billy nodded.

As the coffee pot began to *shssssh* and drip, Mrs. Kenwood said, "Bring your bag, and I'll show you your room."

Billy retrieved his bag and followed her down the cool main hallway.

"I'll give you a tour on the way," she said. "This is the den. The study. The master bedroom. The spare bedroom." She pointed left and right and left again.

The house was as long as a barn—big enough for three families—but everything was so tidy, it looked as if no one lived here. "Archer's room," she said, motioning for Billy to set his bag just inside. Then she turned opposite and opened a door. "And this is my husband's pride and joy, the trophy room."

"I can see why," Billy murmured.

All four walls were covered. There were rows of red, white and blue ribbons hung heavy with medallions. Trophies of all kinds, from basketball to baseball, shone dully on shelf after shelf. "That wall is Mark's, from his college days at Iowa. My husband was a baseball player, too, you know."

"I didn't know that," Billy said. As he squinted at the smaller trophies, some with tarnish on them, he heard the front door slam, and then footsteps.

"That shelf is King's," she continued. "But all the rest are Dick's. You know Dick, our professional baseball player?"

"I've heard about him, yes," Billy said.

"People say that Dick was the best athlete ever to graduate from Flint High," Mrs. Kenwood said.

"They're right," said a man's voice behind, "and he probably always will be."

"Hello, dear! You're home early."

Mark Kenwood stood behind them, gazing at the racks of trophies, the ribbons and plaques. He turned. "I'm not really home yet," he said, glancing at Billy. "I just wanted to make sure you had no trouble getting young Mr. Baggs settled in."

"Why would I have trouble, dear?" his wife said.

Mark Kenwood's eyes flickered up and down his wife. He had the same penetrating gaze, the same thick brown hair as his son. He glanced at his watch. "How long will you be staying?" he asked Billy.

"Until Saturday," Billy mumbled.

Mark Kenwood turned to his wife. "Make sure King gets back into his workout routine. There's no reason why this should disrupt his training."

"I will, dear."

He checked his watch again. "Got to get back to the office."

"What would you like for dinner?" she called after him.

"Whatever," he said, "though I'll probably be a little late. Go ahead without me, but tell King I'll be home in time to work in the cage with him." Checking his watch one more time, Mark Kenwood was gone.

Mrs. Kenwood blinked. "That was the master of house," she said, making a clumsy bow as the front door slammed.

Billy looked away, embarrassed.

She turned back to the trophies, stepping toward a small plaque and photograph near a tattered, faded pom-pom. "This is me," she said.

Billy stepped closer to look.

"I was a cheerleader at Iowa. That's how I met Mark."

Billy nodded.

"I should have been more," she said. "I was smart enough." She fingered the dusty pom-pom as she stared for long moments at the image of several cheerleaders in a pyramid. She pointed. "That's me at the top."

They were both silent.

"Well then, what part of the house haven't we seen?" she said, suddenly turning away from the photo. "Oh yes, the basement."

Billy followed her down carpeted stairs. She flipped a switch, and bright fluorescent lights flickered on. "Also called the gym," she said.

Billy stared. A long white room with floor-length mirrors across the back was lined with sports equipment: bench press, treadmill, stationary bicycle, pull-over machine, leg-squats machine, and other muscle-specific machines he couldn't identify. At the far end of the basement was a wooden ramp covered with tattered green carpet; at the opposite end was a frame covered with stretched netting on which had been painted the silhouette of a right-handed batter.

Billy's eyes traveled back to the ramp. "An inside pitching mound!"

"It's the one Dick used," Mrs. Kenwood said. "We call it the winter mound. Dick used it every night of the snow season. Sometimes he would skip school and spend all day down here, just throwing pitches into the screen. Now King uses it."

Billy stared; then his eyes fell to a clipboard hung on the wall. STRENGTH & CONDITIONING: ARCHER KENWOOD, it read across the top. Below was a grid for the date and number of repetitions for a long list of exercises. It had a place for King to sign, and for his father to initial. The sheet was current except for the past three days.

"His father made that for King," Mrs. Kenwood said, picking up the clipboard, scanning down the list.

Above them the door slammed, and King's voice called out.

"Down here," his mother called.

A grocery sack thudded on the counter; then King came down. He looked at Billy, then at the clipboard.

"Sort of like daily chores," King said.

"I'd say," Billy said.

"Your father said to be sure to—" Mrs. Kenwood began.

"I know, I know," King interrupted, "and he'll miss dinner but be back in time to work out."

His mother shrugged and smiled.

"First I need something to eat," King said.

Upstairs Billy and King had sandwiches and milk. "My, you seem hungrier," Mrs. Kenwood observed.

"Leave us, Mom," King said matter-of-factly.

With a slightly hurt look Mrs. Kenwood disappeared back into the living room, where she turned the television on.

They finished their sandwiches and chocolate milk in silence. King made sure to put everything away and wipe up all the crumbs. Billy was beginning to see the challenge to living in this house: Leave no evidence that you had been here.

"Do you want to work out?" King said.

Billy shrugged. "Not really."

"That's fine. There's a TV in my room. Color," King added.

With the faint sounds of the treadmill in the basement and the clink of ice cubes in the living room, Billy turned on King's TV. The room had bunk beds, tightly made; a study desk, clear except for a reading lamp; baseball posters on one wall, all Nolan Ryan, pinned straight and at equal distances from one another; a covered typewriter on a bench; and no clothes on the floor, not even a stray sock. He flipped on the TV. Images of Vietnam flashed on, then switched to ones of student protests in America. Students were on strike at several universities. He switched channels, found *American Bandstand*. He made sure to keep the volume low.

When the show ended, the rhythmic clink of weights and pulleys continued in the basement. It was getting on toward five o'clock. He was a little hungry again. He listened; there were no sounds from the kitchen. Pausing by King's desk, he ran his fingers slowly across the top. No dust. His hand fell to the widest top drawer. Looking once over his shoulder, he eased it open. A tray with sections for paper clips, rubber bands, pencils, pens, erasers. A place for everything, everything in its place. A fresh tablet was slightly askew in the drawer, and Billy was moved to straighten it. As he did so, he spotted a white page sealed in a clear plastic sleeve. On it was typed: "Personal Goals, High School, Archer Kenwood."

Billy leaned closer and read:

I. Athletics:
    A. Three-year letterman in football, basketball and baseball
        1. Football: running back & quarterback (senior year)
        2. Basketball: guard (45% field goals; 90% free throws)
        3. Baseball: 9th grade, middle reliever;
           10th grade, long reliever, ERA under 3.00
           11th grade, starting pitcher, ERA under 2.00
           12th grade, ace starter, ERA under 1.00

"Good luck," Billy muttered.

II. Academics
    A. Honor Society junior and senior year
    B. Grade point average 3.75 or above
    C. Complete all college prep classes
III. Other
    A. Member, at least two volunteer clubs
    B. Market myself for maximum scholarship offers
    C. Plan future with Suzy

Billy's eyes widened, and at the same time he heard footsteps in the hall. Quickly he closed the desk drawer and leaped back into his chair. King came in, sweating, a white towel looped around his neck.

He squinted at Billy, then looked briefly about the room. "Watching the TV with no sound on?"

Billy shrugged. "I didn't want to disturb anyone."

"Believe me, there's no one to disturb," King said, with a nod toward the living room. He opened a dresser drawer; Billy caught a flash of neatly organized piles of socks and underwear. "I'm going to take a shower; then we'll get supper going."

"Sure," Billy said, letting out a breath as King disappeared down the hall.

As water continued to run in the shower, Billy left King's room and eased down the hall. He peeked into the living room. Mrs. Kenwood, tipped sideways on the couch with a small fan of magazines around her, was breathing softly. The magazines had names he'd never heard of: *Smithsonian, Atlantic Monthly, MacLeans*. He walked on to the kitchen, where he poked about for some food; he opened several cupboard doors but found only glassware and china. Not wishing to get caught snooping, he headed back down the hall.

King emerged from the bathroom in clean jeans and a fresh University of Minnesota sweatshirt. "She sleeping?" he said, jerking his head toward the living room.

Billy nodded.

"Her afternoon nap," King said sarcastically.

"Sure," Billy said quickly.

King passed on to the kitchen. "Spaghetti sound all right for supper?"

"You bet."

And so they set about cooking. King was adept in the kitchen, tearing lettuce, chopping fresh mushrooms and green peppers for a salad; cutting French bread and adding butter and garlic; adding minced garlic to bottled spaghetti sauce in a pan. "We'll turn on the oven broiler and toast that bread all at once," he said.

"Where'd you learn how to cook?" Billy asked, helping wherever he could.

"Right here," King answered. He shook a tall fan of noodles into the bubbling water, pushed them about.

"I've never had to cook anything," Billy said.

"It's not that hard," King said, tossing the salad with long wooden spoons. "If you can read, you can cook. It's just a matter of following the recipes."

As they set the table, King said, "What do you want to do after dinner?"

Billy shrugged.

"I usually play an hour of yard ball, then study."

"Okay."

The two of them finally sat down to eat. There were cloth napkins and two forks. Billy watched King to see which fork he used for the salad—the little one. Midway through dinner Mrs. Kenwood suddenly appeared. "Well how sweet, the two of you eating together."

"You should eat something," King said.

"I'm not real hungry, but I'll join you," she said.

King frowned as his mother poured a glass of red wine. Then she sat down with them and picked at a small bowl of salad.

"This is very good," she said.

"What—the salad or the wine?"

"The salad, dear, of course," she said, looking hurt.

King was silent for a few bites.

"When we're done, Billy and I are going to do some yard ball, then study."

"Did you work out? Your father asked me—"

"I worked out!" King said.

His mother flinched at her son's voice. "I only asked."

They ate on in silence. When he was done, Billy carefully took his plate to the sink. "Just put it in the dishwasher," King said.

"Be sure to rinse it well first," King's mother added.

Billy ran water over his plate, then held it and looked around the kitchen again.

"The dishwasher," King said from over by the refrigerator.

"Where's the dishwasher?" Billy mumbled.

King's mother stared, then let out a brief laugh.

"Shut up," King said sharply to her. "How's he supposed to know everything?"

"I'm sorry, dear," Mrs. Kenwood said, touching her mouth. "I just never thought that someone wouldn't know—"

"Well, he doesn't know," King interrupted, stalking across the kitchen to pull down a wide paneled door. He pointed inside, to the racks that slid on little wheels. "The plates stand up here, glasses and cups there, silverware in that little tray. We add soap, and the machine does the rest."

Billy nodded.

"I didn't mean to insult our guest," King's mother continued.

"We're going out now," King said sharply.

After changing into his tennis shoes, Billy followed King into the backyard. King carried a whole duffel bag of balls. Outside, Billy stared at a long, narrow batting cage built of tall poles and black netting. At one end was a well-worn batter's box and scuffed plate; at the other end was a portable screen fronting a tripod covered by a waterproof tarp. It was a better cage than the one at the school field.

King dropped his glove and stretched. Self-consciously Billy leaned against the cage. In the September evening air he looked around. Past low hedges and picket fences, two lawn mowers hummed, children played, dogs romped, smoke drifted from barbecue grills. There was no work in sight, not a single chore to do. And only three houses down was Suzy Langen's ranch house; once he was sure he heard her laughter.

Two small neighborhood boys, spotting King, ran up to the fence. "Hey, King! Can I run the pitching machine?"

"No, me, King!" the other shouted.

"Sorry guys, I got somebody for tonight."

The boys stuck out their lower lips at Billy, then raced off.

"Pests," King called. "In some ways you're lucky to live in the country."

Billy looked again across the pleasant evening backyards.

King headed into the cage, where he yanked off the tarp to reveal a blue pitching machine, the newer kind with two rubber wheels that pinched the ball between them and spit it forward. It was a much nicer machine than the school's old long-armed thrower.

"Want to hit?" King asked.

Billy shrugged. "Okay." He found a hefty aluminum bat and stretched his back muscles while King made sure the machine was plugged in.

King adjusted some dials. "Ready?"

Billy nodded and dug in at the plate.

The smudged yellow ball whizzed past Billy's chest like a grouse exploding from its perch in a tree; Billy felt the air on his face but never got the bat off his shoulder.

"Jesus; how fast was that?" Billy asked, stepping out.

"Ninety-five."

"I hardly even saw it!"

"That's how it's gonna be in the big leagues," King said.

"Let me try another one," Billy said. This time he whiffed cleanly.

"Slow it down? Maybe to college level?"

Billy shook his head stubbornly. "Ready," he said. This time, by stepping forward at nearly the same time as King's hand moved, he fouled the yellow streaker straight back.

"Decent cut," King allowed.

"One more fast one," Billy said, glancing down at the positioning of his feet. He did not notice King adjusting the dials.

When he swung this time, the ball was much yellower, much sharper and altogether larger: He was confident of crushing it. The ball was also ten miles per hour slower, and Billy stumbled forward as he whiffed at it.

There was laughter, a man's laughter, from behind the screen. "That would be Nolan Ryan's change-up," Mark Kenwood said. He was home from work, still dressed in shirt and tie. "I'll get changed and be right out," he said.

"You bat," Billy said to King, and stepped out.

"No, no, stay in there. I'll stop fooling around," King said. He turned the dials again. "Standard seventy miles per hour for batting practice."

Billy's first few swings were off-balance and stiff.

"You're pulling your head out. Watch the ball onto the bat," King said. He kept working with Billy, who, after adjusting his stance, gradually loosened up and began to drive the balls, one after another. Mark Kenwood returned in his sweat suit just as King ducked, and a ball banged off the blue metal pipe. "That's what you get for helping him," Mark Kenwood muttered to his son.

King shrugged.

"Step out of there, kid; we've got work to do," Mark Kenwood called to Billy. He gestured for Billy to leave. Billy ducked under the netting as Mark Kenwood took over the pitching machine. "Your turn, King."

King found a bat. Billy leaned against the fence to watch.

As his father fed the balls into the machine, King stood like a robot and smashed ball after ball straightaway. Swing away ten times, bunt twice, swing away again. King's bat went *tock, tock, tock* like the pendulum on a large clock.

"Good wood, King," a girl's voice called.

They all turned.

Suzy Langen approached from the opposite side of the fence.

"I heard the noise," she said pleasantly. She had on shorts and a Northwestern University sweatshirt, and her hair was pulled back.

"Ah . . . hullo," the boys mumbled. King glanced sideways at Billy, then motioned for his father to resume. Suzy leaned on the pickets by Billy; they watched in silence. King whiffed on the next ball, then fouled off the next two.

"Come on, focus!" Mark called.

"They do this every night," Suzy murmured as King grunted and swung. "Whack, whack, whack. Before King it was his brother. Whack, whack, whack, every evening. Most of Saturday and Sunday. It's one of the neighborhood sounds that's imprinted on my brain."

Billy nodded. He tried not to look at her. Also, King was suddenly having great difficulty at the plate.

"Watch the ball all the way onto the bat!" Mark said.

"I am, I am," King replied, pounding the plate once with his bat.

Suzy said, "Did you meet his mother?"

"Kind of," Billy murmured.

"Mother Kind Of is right. The sad thing is that she wanted to go to law school, but then she married you know who. When she gets really drunk, she talks about going back to school."

"She could," Billy said. "My ma went out and got a job."

In the cage Mark Kenwood stared down at King.

"Step out and refocus if you need to," he called. "Don't let me dictate the rhythm. Assert yourself in the box, for God's sakes."

King pivoted one foot out, took a deep breath. As his son looked away, Mark Kenwood cranked a dial, and then King stepped back in. The next pitch, much slower, broke down and in, and King screwed himself nearly into the ground as he flailed at it.

"Curve! Curve! You got to keep your weight back; you know that!"

King hammered the ground hard with his bat, then reset himself.

"And you thought your father was tough," Suzy murmured. Billy looked sideways at her.

King whiffed at the next two pitches, then tossed the bat aside, toward Billy. "Your turn," he said angrily.

"Get back in there, dammit," Mark said. "Never stop on a whiff!"

"I'd better go," Suzy said to King. "I don't want to interrupt your fun—if that's what you're having."

"Wait," King said to her.

"Ability to focus separates the men from the boys," Mark said.

King turned away from Suzy and angrily picked up the bat and swept it over the plate; he readied himself for the next pitch.

Mark Kenwood fed the ball, and King crushed it, sending a line drive just inches off his father's right ear.

"Good!" his father called, and fed another ball.

Suzy stared. Then she said to Billy, "You know what separates the men from the boys—at least with you guys and your fathers?"

"No. What?" Billy said.

"Nothing," she said. She turned sharply away, and her ponytail waved good-bye.

That evening Billy tried to study at the same time as King. But King's concentration unnerved him. Billy could never sit still and read for more than ten minutes straight; King did not move until he had finished a whole chapter. Billy fidgeted. Checked his watch.

"You need something?" King said with irritation.

"No," Billy said, and refocused on his English.

King rustled a page. They read for some time. "So what did Suzy want?" King asked.

Billy shrugged. "Nothing, I guess. Just being neighborly."

King had no comment.

That night Billy lay in a firm bed on faintly perfumed, very tight sheets. He could hear cars on occasion, and several dogs yapping in the distance. The roof did not creak with comforting sounds. He shifted this way and that, searching for a channel, a groove that fit his body, like his mattress at home.

"By the way, sorry about my old man tonight," King said.

"What for?"

"The way he put you out of the cage."

"No big deal."

King was silent for a space. "He takes his baseball very seriously."

"I noticed," Billy said.

They lay there in silence for a while.

"Actually he takes my baseball very seriously," King said. "He wants me to be a college pitcher, then try out for the pros."

"Like your brother," Billy said.

"Or else like himself, only younger."

"I saw his trophies from college days."

"He was a good athlete," King said. "He had a tryout with the Cardinals, but he didn't catch on. It was my brother who made it, at least so far."

Billy lay there in the dark for a while. "In my family Robert was the star. He could do anything. Read when he was four. Good at every sport he tried."

"You'd be good at every sport," King said.

"No way," Billy said. "I play basketball like a clubfoot. I'm too skinny for football. Baseball's my thing."

King was silent.

The following day in school, Billy sat with King's group. He had made sure to wear his real clothes:

jeans, cowboy boots and a black T-shirt. The madras shirts, the slacks, the penny loafers, remained at home in the back of his closet. It had been a stupid idea in the first place, buying clothes for someone he wasn't. King led the way through the cafeteria. He made sure they didn't sit near Suzy, who seemed happy to stay at the far end of the table.

"So, Billy Baggs, how do you like life in the big city?" Doug Nixon asked.

Billy shrugged. "It's okay."

"Okay? You mean you aren't homesick?"

Billy settled into his seat. All eyes turned his way. "Well, I do miss one thing," he said.

"What's that?"

"Here in town I can't step out in the front yard and take a piss."

The table erupted in laughter, most of it directed toward Doug, whose smile slipped. Suzy grinned broadly and looked down at her tray.

"Hey King, your old man's shrubs are all gonna turn brown and die!" Doug said, trying for an even bigger laugh, but no one joined him. Billy kept eating, and soon the college prep crowd left him alone. They talked about ACT and SAT tests, about traveling to the Twin Cities and to Chicago. It was as if he was in a different country. King didn't have much to say to anyone.

During the next two days his and King's best moments were centered upon food—either eating together or cooking at King's house. Food kept them occupied, and if King gave directions, Billy was happy to help prepare the meals; otherwise, where was the food going to come from? He quickly learned a good deal about cooking.

They also had, after supper, some reasonably good times in the batting cage. If Billy was lucky, he got in fifty or so swings at the plate before Mark Kenwood came home. When King's father showed up, it was clear that three was a crowd. Billy vamoosed, then leaned on the fence and watched King's workout. Four was even more of a crowd; Suzy did not come across the yards again.

On Friday night, as they headed outside, King said, "The machine puts the ball in the same spot, at the same speed every time. You want to do some live batting practice?"

"Sure," Billy said, taking the ball bag. He was happy to throw. From no chores, no work, his muscles had begun to feel hidebound, his blood as thick as winter oil in a cold tractor. He was halfway through a second bag of balls and starting a pleasing sweat, his arm getting that comfortably loosey-goosey feeling, when Mark Kenwood appeared.

"What are you doing?" Mark called loudly to King. He still wore his suit and tie.

"Batting practice; what does it look like?"

"Use the machine!" Mark Kenwood said. "I don't want you getting hurt."

"I'm not throwing full speed," Billy said.

"I asked him to pitch. He's mixing them up so I can work on my timing."

Mark Kenwood watched in silence. Billy grooved

ball after ball, at various speeds, and King hammered them straight away. "Good," Mark said. Then, "Way to wait on it. That's it." He soon disappeared and returned in his sweat suit.

"Live batting practice is the only way to go," King said to Billy. "Give me another half dozen."

Billy obliged. Afterward, stepping out to catch his breath, King turned to his father. "You want to hit some?"

"Me?" Mark said.

"Why not? You haven't hit any all week."

Mark shrugged.

"He's just lobbing them," King added.

"All right. Let me loosen up my old bones first." Billy continued throwing while King's father went through the same stretching that King used. Mark Kenwood put on a batting helmet and stepped in.

"He hit .324 at Iowa," King called to Billy.

"That was a while ago," Mark Kenwood said.

"Don't let him kid you," King said. "In the summer he plays fast-pitch softball every night of the week. He hammers those Blue Dots into orbit."

Billy lobbed a pitch full over the plate. Mark Kenwood uncoiled on it, and Billy had to duck below the short screen as the ball screamed past.

"See what I mean?" King said.

His father crushed the next three balls in similar fashion.

"Put a little more on it," Mark said.

Billy pitched slightly faster with each group of balls. Soon King's father was fouling or missing altogether. He cursed whenever he missed. This was not a good scene, but luckily Billy was nearly done with the bag. He slowed down on the next couple of pitches.

"What are you slacking off for?" Mark called.

"You think I've never seen a fastball?"

Billy shrugged. He held up the last ball. "One left. This is it."

"Show me your best stuff, kid," Mark said. Sweat shone on his forehead; he poised his bat behind his neck and tensed at the plate.

Billy took his full windup and threw his high heat straight down the pike. Mark Kenwood never moved. The ball hissed past him untouched, then tore through the back of the netting and trickled across the lawn. "Jesus Christ," Mark murmured. He looked behind at the hole in the cage.

"Sorry!" Billy said quickly.

On the sidelines King grinned at his father, then trotted after the ball.

At that moment King's mother appeared at the patio door. "Phone for you, Archer!"

"Tell them he's busy!" Mark said angrily, and tossed aside the bat.

"It's his grandmother. It won't hurt him to talk for a couple of minutes."

King flipped the ball back toward the cage and dutifully trotted inside. Billy was left in silence with Mark Kenwood.

"I'll tie up the netting," Billy volunteered.

"I said don't worry about it!" Kenwood answered,

not looking at Billy. He began to gather balls, tossing them one by one into the open bag. Billy helped him.

Gradually, as they recovered the balls, they were only a couple of steps apart. Kenwood stood up and glanced at the house, then turned to Billy. "So, kid, what are your baseball plans?"

Billy let his shoulders rise and fall. "I dunno."

"But you plan on playing high-school ball?"

"Yeah. Probably."

"For Flint?"

"Where else?" Billy said, surprised.

"You could play for Buckman," Kenwood said, stooping for a ball. "From your farm, west, it's about the same distance as you drive to Flint, isn't it?"

"I guess," Billy said, "but I don't know anybody in Buckman."

"Buckman's a nice little town," Mark Kenwood said. "I know quite a few people over there, including the coach, Rick Allen, a great guy, by the way. I even know a couple of doctors over at the Buckman Clinic—it's a fine clinic, they say."

Billy stared, puzzled.

Luckily, King returned, and Billy was free of his father. He watched Mark Kenwood from the fence.

The only thing missing in King's cage was a bank of floodlights, and that was because the neighbors would revolt, Suzy had said. At sundown they called it quits. After King headed to the shower, Billy was watching King's television when Mark Kenwood appeared in the doorway. "I understand that your father is coming to pick you up tomorrow morning?"

"That's right."

"What time?"

"Ten o'clock."

"Would you call him and tell him I'd like to speak to him when he comes—a friendly, man-to-man kind of talk?" Mark said. He produced his half smile.

"I suppose," Billy said, "though I don't know how much talking he'll want to do with you."

"Tell him I'm sure he'll want to talk to me."

"Okay," Billy said skeptically. Mark Kenwood left the room. Billy stared at King's phone. It would be a cold day in hell before Abner would want to talk with Mark Kenwood; on the other hand, maybe if the two fathers did talk, they could get past some things. Like Billy had with King. He would never be King's friend—too much divided them—but he didn't necessarily have to be King's enemy. If he had learned anything from Coach Anderson's experiment, it was that he and King didn't have to like each other, but they did have to tolerate one another. Sometimes tolerable was enough. Billy had a flash of an idea that maybe a lot of times in life, tolerable was enough. He picked up the phone and dialed home.

On Saturday morning he and King had cereal and toast. King's mother was still sleeping, his father *thud-thudd*ing on the treadmill in the basement. Billy himself was weirdly exhausted, as if he had filled silo for a week, or cut a train-car load of pulp wood. "Do you want coffee?" King said, glancing at him. "I forgot that you liked coffee."

"I don't really," Billy said.

King paused to look at Billy. "Sorry about my mom this week."

Billy shrugged. "No problem."

"Actually, she has a problem," King said. "She's a boozer. An alcoholic."

Billy looked down into his cereal bowl.

"I keep trying to get her to get some help. Maybe she will. Someday."

They ate on in silence. King changed the subject. "So, Baggs. As your father might say, what's your verdict on life in the suburbs?"

Billy thought a moment. "It's okay, but . . ."

"But what?"

Billy thought. "I'm not sure. Maybe it's that the suburbs give the impression that life is easy. Easier, I mean, than it really is."

King looked at him. "Did you know that you're a lot smarter than you think?"

"Gee, thanks," Billy said dryly.

After they had tidied the dishes and run the dishwasher, Billy packed up and set his bag by the front door. Abner was due soon.

Billy and King sat in the white living room to wait. A wall clock ticked. King turned on the television, but it was only cartoons, and he switched it off.

Mark Kenwood came in, checking his watch. "I want you guys outside when Mr. Baggs arrives. We'll need some privacy to talk."

Billy and King looked at each other. "Sure," King said, shrugging. His father seemed annoyed that neither of them moved.

As Mark disappeared, Billy said, "I wonder what they're going to talk about."

"Me too," King said.

"Maybe it's something about my old man's probation."

King was briefly silent. "Your father hasn't done anything wrong recently. Has he?"

"No," Billy replied. "Nothing."

"Then maybe it's good news of some kind."

"Yeah. Maybe so." Outside the morning sunlight looked suddenly brighter. Billy had a surge of hope—hope that his father was not going to do any more crazy things, hope that things were changing. He was so optimistic that his stomach did not clench and his heart did not skip a beat at the sound of the Baggses' family pickup rattling to a stop out front.

"Out!" Mark Kenwood said suddenly to them from the living-room doorway.

"We're going, we're going," King said. Rather than go outside, they went to King's room and closed the door. They waited. Billy sat on the bed.

Soon there was heavy thudding on the front door.

"Why couldn't he use the damn doorbell?" Billy said.

"Because your house doesn't have one," King said.

Billy glanced at King and had to nod his agreement. Then both boys turned their ears toward muffled voices in the foyer.

"Jesus Christ," Mark Kenwood said.

"You wanted to see me, right?" Abner said.

"Well, yes, but—"

"So here I am."

"Do you want to take off your boots, at least?" Mark said.

"No time for that. I just came from the barn. As you might guess, I've been a little shorthanded the last few days."

"Oh, Christ," Billy said, and dropped his forehead to his hands.

"What?" King whispered.

"You don't want to know."

King eased open his door and peeked down the hall. Only seconds later Billy could smell manure wafting down the hall. Fresh cow manure. He knew without looking that Abner had come dressed in barn coveralls and with shit on his boots.

"At least . . . wipe your feet," Mark Kenwood said.

"Sure, no problem," Abner said. Billy could hear his father's boots stomp and drag.

"My mother's good rug!" King breathed.

"Damn him," Billy said. He started toward the door, but King blocked his path.

"No, wait. We've got to let them talk."

Billy let out a deep angry breath and turned away.

"They're going into the kitchen," King said.

Billy sat back on the bed and put his head in his hands. He just wanted this to be over. He just wanted to go home. King leaned into the hallway to listen. The two fathers' voices were muffled and indistinct.

"Let's go outside, along the house. We could hear what they're saying," King said.

"I don't know if I want to."

"I do," King said.

Billy followed. King eased out through the back door, then went around the side of the house. The men's voices grew more distinct. King motioned for Billy to join him beneath the kitchen window. They crouched there.

". . . and what I'm saying is, you've got this probation thing hanging over your head—which is not fun, I'm sure." King's father was speaking.

King glanced at Billy encouragingly.

"And I've got my own problems," Mark Kenwood continued. "Well, only one, really. My son, Archer. He's a good baseball player, and works real hard, but he'll never measure up to his brother."

King froze.

"On the other hand, if he works hard he could be Coach Anderson's ace in high school, and probably get a scholarship, though I doubt at the Division One level. He doesn't really have that kind of talent," Mark Kenwood said.

King's face began to pale.

"But the key thing in baseball—in any sport, really—is to make your mark in high school. To be the go-to-guy, the one in the papers, the team leader."

"So what's that got to do with me?" Abner Baggs said.

"I was talking the other day with Rick Allen, the baseball coach over at Buckman High School. He's real enthusiastic about your son as a pitcher."

"Wait a minute—"

"And I know that other kids from your side of the county go to Buckman High—it's their choice, right?"

King's face turned ashen. He glanced at the ground as if he would like to leave but couldn't move his feet.

"Are you saying you want my son to go Buckman so that your boy can be a star pitcher here at Flint?" Abner's voice grew louder by the word.

"Wait, hear me out."

Abner was silent. Billy could feel his father's anger pulsing, radiating out the window, spilling over the sill.

"If you transferred Billy to Buckman High, I'd talk to Judge Langen. Between the judge and me, we could make your probation problem go away. You'd be free and clear in Flint County."

King turned away and slumped against the side of the house, his legs outstretched. He stared across the yard at the batting cage, the silent pitching machine.

"You might even want to appeal that six-thousand-dollar restitution to Randy Meyers," Mark continued, hurrying now. "Who knows? You might get some of that money back. You play ball with me and the judge, and only good things can happen to you."

Billy heard a soft, low croaking sound that grew into a hoarse, rhythmic bark. It was Abner laughing.

"What's so damn funny?" Mark Kenwood said.

"Of all the . . ." Abner began. He was overcome by rasping, wheezing laughter.

"You don't think that things work this way?" Kenwood said.

"Oh, I know they do," Abner choked out. "I've known that for years."

"Well, here's your chance to get on board."

"And here's your chance to kiss my ass!" Abner said. There was a sudden large crash—the sound of a chair tipping over, then being kicked against a wall. His voice was suddenly clear and enormously angry.

Billy looked at King. "I gotta go!" he whispered hoarsely. "I got to get him out of here."

King nodded vacantly. He was on his feet now, heading toward the cage but walking oddly, as if he was sleepwalking. Billy hurried inside the house.

"If you think you can run my son out of this school, if you think you can buy me off with some backroom deal, you're even more crooked than I thought."

"Nobody's being run out or bought off. It's

just . . . an arrangement. I'm just trying to do what's best for my son."

"Pa, come on. Let's go home," Billy said from the doorway.

Abner looked briefly at Billy but didn't really see him. He was focused on Kenwood.

"If you think that's best for your son, if you think that's the way to raise him, why . . . why he'd be better off if you went out and shot yourself."

Mark Kenwood's face went white, then red. "You're telling me how to raise a son? You, the guy who can't even take care of the kids he had?"

"Why you sonofabitch!" Abner said. He lunged at Mark Kenwood, but Billy grabbed his father by the arm and spun him toward the door.

"Get out!" Kenwood shouted.

"We are, we are!" Billy called, grabbing his bag and pushing his father ahead of him.

Outside, Abner swore over his shoulder at the Kenwood house.

"Keep going, come on," Billy said, moving him to the truck. The cooler air and bright sunlight helped Abner get himself under control.

"Want me to drive?" Billy said.

"No. I can drive, for God's sakes." Abner got behind the wheel. He turned to Billy. "Did you hear what he wanted me to do?"

"Yes, but it doesn't matter right now. Let's just go home."

Abner stared at the steering wheel, then started the engine. Then his eyes turned to the Kenwoods' wide, perfect front lawn. His pupils began to gleam.

"Don't, Pa," Billy said immediately.

Abner ignored him. With a roar from the engine, he bounced the pickup over the curb and spun its tires on a wide, slewing circle across the lawn. Mud and green sod chunks flew. A shrub tore loose under the bumper and thrashed along underneath. Billy grabbed the wheel and yanked the truck back toward the street. The tires clunked back over the curb and left muddy strips on the clean asphalt. Behind, the Kenwoods' yard was left with Abner's swirling dark signature.

At home Mavis had a big noon meal ready: fried chicken, potatoes, gravy, pie. Billy ate quietly. "I thought you'd be more hungry," his mother said. Abner, head down, chewed on in silence.

"It's so good, I'm taking my time," Billy said, trying to muster a happy face.

His mother smiled and passed a steaming bowl of potatoes. "So things went all right at the Kenwood house?"

"Sure," he said quickly; he glanced toward his father.

Abner had no comment.

"Did Pa get on all right with the chores?" Billy said. By blunting the edge of his father's anger, he was trying to put on a good front—a family front—for his mother. It was something that he did often, he realized.

"Not really," Abner muttered.

"We had Big Danny over for a couple of days," Mavis said.

"How'd he do?" Billy asked. There he went again. After being away at King's house, he could now hear himself, even see himself from outside his own body. Here he was, worrying about how his father would react to this or to that. Here he was, trying to build bridges to the cold island where his father lived.

"Average. And not on the high side of average," Abner said.

"He did fine," Mavis said. "He's a good worker. We should have him more often."

"Gives me the creeps. Never says a word all day," Abner said. "You try working with somebody like that."

Billy looked down at his food. Home a half hour, and already he was starting to feel defensive about being alive.

"Let's just eat, shall we?" Mavis said. "We're finally all home, together. That's the good thing."

Then the phone rang. Billy flinched. Abner looked his way.

"Everything all right?" Mavis asked.

"Sure," Billy said quickly, though he was sure it was the sheriff, calling for Abner, calling about the Kenwoods' lawn. Now they would come and take his father away again, and—

"Just answer it," Abner said.

Mavis picked up the receiver on the third ring. "Hello? . . . It's for you, Billy."

Billy glanced at Abner.

"A girl," his mother added. Abner's grim expression lightened toward an actual smile, and as it did, Mavis's face turned as angry as Billy had ever seen it. He quickly pulled the phone around into the pantry.

"Hello?"

"Billy, it's Suzy."

He glanced around the corner at his parents, who had begun to crank up their voices in argument.

"Hi!" he said, still surprised.

"Listen, what went on at King's when you were there?"

"Kind of what you saw. You know, a lot of hanging around the cage. Though it got a little ugly at the end."

"Well that's why I called. I was just out in the yard and I kept hearing this sawing sound. You know, like somebody sawing down a tree. I went over to the fence to look, and the sound was coming from King's yard. He was out there with a hand saw, sawing down his batting cage."

"Jesus!" Billy murmured.

"His father was shouting at him, but he couldn't get close because of the way King was swinging the saw. It was crazy. King was crazy. He went on like a robot. All the neighbors came out to watch. Pretty soon the whole cage came crashing down. It smashed the fence and everything. Can you believe it?"

Billy was silent. "Yes. I can," he said softly. Then, after making her promise not to tell anyone, he explained what had happened between his father and Mark Kenwood. He explained how he and King had heard everything; how Abner and Mark Kenwood had gotten crazy; how Abner had spun the truck tires on the Kenwoods' lawn. When he was finished, Suzy was silent for a moment.

"The whole thing is nuts," she murmured.

"No kidding."

"You and King have to do something."

"Like what?"

"Like with your fathers."

Billy was silent.

"Don't you see what's going on?" she asked.

Billy shrugged, then realized that Suzy couldn't hear a shrug. "Kind of," he said.

"I'm sure it's tough to see because you're both so close to it," she went on, "and maybe I shouldn't intrude—"

"Hey, it can't get much worse," Billy replied.

Suzy paused. "All right, here goes: It's your fathers. Maybe deep down they're good men, but they're really screwing you over. The rest of the world is moving on, but you and King are stuck. And you'll stay that way until you do something about them."

"Like what?"

"I don't know. Go on strike," she said.

"Say again?"

"Sorry. Just trying for a small laugh here."

"You said go on strike—"

"I was just reading the newspaper, you know, student protests at the University of Minnesota because of Vietnam. People all over keep going on strike for various reasons, so why couldn't sons go on strike from their fathers?" She laughed briefly.

Billy was silent.

"Hello?" Suzy said.

"I'm thinking," Billy murmured.

"Well, think out loud."

"The coach," Billy said suddenly. "We've got to get in touch with Coach Anderson."

"Who does? Why?"

"Me and King," Billy said, "we have to. Hey, thanks, Suzy, I'll talk to you in school on Monday."

"Wait, what's going on?"

"Everything," Billy said. "I'll explain later."

That evening, when Mavis and Abner were outside, Billy dialed the coach's phone number.

Coach Anderson answered on the second ring, and Billy launched his plan with hardly a "hello."

"Hey wait! Is that you, Billy? Slow down," the coach said.

Billy took a breath and started over.

The coach listened. Occasionally he said, "I hear you," or "You've got that right." Billy told the coach about Mark Kenwood's Buckman bribe offer; Coach Anderson was not surprised. "Go on," he said.

"So," Billy said at the end. "What do you think?"

The coach let out a breath. "It's dramatic," he said. He fell silent. "But then again, maybe it's the only thing that will work."

"So will you help us?"

"In for a penny, in for a pound. Yes. We'll do it in my homeroom right after school on Monday."

Monday morning, as the bus pulled up, Darrel Wind and Gina called out warnings to Billy. "Hey, it's Kenwood. He's waiting for you."

"Rumble time!" someone called.

"Where's his gang?" someone else said.

"One-on-one, you can take him, Billy!"

Billy ignored them. On the sidewalk, King came up to the bus. His face was drawn, and there were bags under his eyes as if he hadn't slept much. They stared at each other.

"You think we're crazy?" Billy said.

"I don't know," King said, "but I got my list."

"Me too," Billy said.

The day passed with agonizing slowness. At lunch neither Billy nor King, who sat apart at their old tables, ate much. They kept glancing at each other or else at the clock. In shop class Billy was lucky not to grind off his fingers as he worked on his handy belt-loop worm can. Afterward, in the hallway before their last class, the coach stopped both boys in the hall. "Well, I made the calls," he said.

Billy and King looked at each other.

"There's no turning back now," Coach Anderson said. There was a gleam in his eyes, a spring in his step, as if they were headed into the last inning of a tough ball game.

During English class Suzy kept glancing at Billy and King as they fidgeted and checked the clock. King bit his fingernails almost continuously. Billy was certain that Miss Henderson would spot their edginess and call on them for sure, but she didn't. When the bell rang, King and Billy turned to look at each other. The other students, except for Suzy, hustled out.

"Good luck, boys," Miss Henderson said as she turned to clean the blackboard. "I think you're doing the right thing."

Billy and King stared at each other.

"What's going on?" Suzy whispered.

Billy blinked. "You said we should do something."

"So we are," King added.

"You can listen through the door if you want," Billy said. "Coach Anderson's room. Right now."

The three of them passed down the hallway. There were already loud voices from behind the coach's closed door. Through the little glass window Billy saw his father and Mark Kenwood. They stood on opposite sides of the coach's desk; behind the coach, who was seated, were his usual blackboards full of tidy handwritten lesson plans. Suzy drew in a breath.

"What's the meaning of this?" Mark Kenwood said. "I was led to believe there was some kind of emergency."

"Me too," Abner Baggs said angrily.

"I'd say it is a kind of emergency," the coach said quietly. He peered toward the door, looking for Billy and King.

"Now or never," King whispered.

Billy nodded, and they pushed through the door.

"There they are, all in one piece. I want to know what's going on!" Mark Kenwood said.

"What's going on is that we're on strike," Billy said.

The room quieted. The fathers turned to their sons.

"As of right now," King said, glancing at the wall clock. "Three thirty-two P.M."

"Huh? What?" Mark Kenwood and Abner Baggs said.

"What we mean," King said, "is that we're on strike as your sons."

There was absolute silence in the room. Abner Baggs sat down; Mark Kenwood followed suit.

"Will somebody tell me what's going on?" Mark murmured.

"Well," the coach said, "they just told you. They're on strike as your sons. Temporarily they are declaring themselves not your sons."

Both fathers turned their gaze on the coach. Abner's dark eyes began to blaze.

"Don't look at me," the coach said quickly. "I've got nothing to do with this. The last thing I want to do is intrude in your family life. I'm just providing some space for you and your boys to work this out."

"Work what out?" Mark said. He seemed less angry than dazed.

"The strike," Billy said.

"How can you go on strike as my son?" Mark said, turning to King. "You *are* my son."

"The point is, a lot of the time I wish I wasn't," King said. He swallowed.

"That goes for me, too," Billy said. He met his father's gaze.

Abner and Mark turned to each other.

"Don't get us wrong; we're glad to have fathers," King said. "A lot of kids, like Tim and Butch, don't have dads."

"But we want changes," Billy followed.

"Big changes," King said.

The two fathers stared at their sons, then again at the coach. He held up his hands, palms out, as if helpless to intercede.

"In fact, we each have a list of what we want changed," King said. Billy and King took sheets of paper from their shirt pockets and handed them to the coach.

"They asked me to read them," the coach said. "That all right with you two?"

The two fathers sat dumbly.

"Okay; here's Billy's list. Number one, he wants—"

"Let me guess," Abner interrupted, as if coming out of a trance. "He wants out of some of his chores. He thinks I work him too hard. What he doesn't know is that hard work—"

"Yes, it's about work," the coach said, "and I have to say that I agree with Billy on this one. Many a time I've seen him dozing in my classes, even in the dugout, because he's gotten up four hours before anyone else and done more work in one day

219

than most town kids do in a month."

Abner glared at the coach but stayed quiet.

"Some kind of hired help to take some of the pressure off Billy's workload at home," the coach said. "Not all of his chores, but a few of them; that's what he's asking."

"Anyway, I told you so," Abner said to Mark.

"They wouldn't do anything if we didn't push them," Mark replied.

"But that's only number one," the coach said.

Abner blinked.

"Number two has to do with, I quote, 'you being mad all the time,'" the coach read.

Abner narrowed his eyes.

Billy swallowed. "What I mean there," he began, "is that you can't know how bad I feel, Pa, when you're pissed off all the time. And most of the time I don't even know what you're pissed at. So I go around feeling like I've done something wrong—and Ma does that too—and pretty soon it's like you've sucked all the oxygen out of the room and we can't breathe. . . ."

Abner, looking confused, stared at his son.

The coach said quietly, "You do have a hair trigger for a temper, Abner. I've seen it myself."

Abner bit his lower lip and looked down briefly. When his eyes returned to the coach, they carried renewed anger. "So how many more on the list?"

"Just one more. Number three: 'One family vehicle is not enough. Since we live twenty miles from town, we need more than just the pickup. And I know for a fact that we can afford at least a used car.'"

"Guess who's looking forward to his driver's license," Abner remarked to King's father.

"It's not for me, it's for Ma," Billy said immediately. "She had her own car, and then you got pissed off because it was a lemon so you destroyed Meyers's car lot, but that wasn't the worst of it. The worst of it was you never let her get another car, so now she has to depend on either you or that old biddy, Mrs. Pederson, for rides to and from work. How do you think that must make Ma feel?"

A frown grew between Abner's eyes; their gaze flickered uncertainly.

"Some hired help, more kindness, a used car," the coach said. "A reasonable list, Abner, I've got to say."

Abner Baggs looked at Mark Kenwood.

"Okay, next," the coach said.

Mark swallowed as the coach began to read.

"Number one, not necessarily in order of importance: 'Please stop embarrassing me at sporting events.'"

Mark looked puzzled.

King addressed his father. "I hate it when I'm on the mound and you're shouting at the umpire on every call, or when I'm playing basketball and you're screaming at the ref. It's the same thing, every sport. Why do you think I bite my fingernails? Why do you think I throw up before most games? It's not because I'm nervous about competing. It's because

I'm worried about how you're going to behave."

Mark looked pained.

"I've got to agree with that," the coach said. "Do you remember earlier this summer, when Sheriff Olson had to handcuff you to a hay wagon so we could finish a Farm Team game?"

Mark looked to the floor, then glanced up at his son. "It's just that I want you to do well."

"Fine; but I could probably do even better without you going crazy and making a fool of yourself," King said.

Mark hardened his gaze. "What's number two?"

"Second and last," the coach read, "'I'm not my brother, Dick. I'll never be Dick. Stop trying to make me into Dick.'"

Mark shifted in his desk.

"I heard everything you said about my 'talent,'" King said, anger rising in his voice. "So maybe I'm not Division One caliber. I still like the game."

His father looked down.

Abner, who had regained some of his edge, spoke up. "So this strike of yours," he said. "What are you boys going to do if we don't happen to agree with your ideas?"

Billy and King looked at each other.

Billy spoke first. "King and I talked that over. For my part, I would stop doing chores. No milking, no cleaning the gutter, no nothing. You'd be in a bind real quick."

"And you'd be out on your ass real quick, looking for another roof over your head," Abner said.

"I talked with Butch Redbird. I can live with him and his mother."

Abner swallowed; his eyes flickered to the Kenwoods.

"As for me," King began, "I would stop playing high school sports altogether."

"What!" Mark exclaimed.

"You heard me," King said. "Done. *Finito.*"

Coach Anderson winced.

"So what the hell would you do if you weren't in sports?" his father said derisively. "Join the damn band?"

"Why not?" King replied. "The guys in band and choir aren't dumb. While Billy and I are busting our asses at ball practice or in the batting cages, those guys are doing stuff with all the best girls."

"Yeah," Billy said suddenly. He had never thought of that before.

Mark Kenwood bit his lower lip; he glanced toward Abner Baggs. Both fathers were silent. Then Abner spoke.

"To sum up," he said with sarcasm, "you two boys think you're so smart that you don't need to listen to your fathers anymore."

"That's not it," King said. "We just need you to step out of our way."

"Let us figure things out for ourselves, like you had to. Let us be who we are, not who you want us to be," Billy finished.

The fathers were both silent again. A deep, spacious silence this time. On the wall the clock's second hand moved with a steady click.

Click.

Click.

Coach Anderson cleared his throat. "I really do need these boys on the team," he said.

Leaving the coach's homeroom, Abner and Billy walked along the empty halls toward the main door. The sound of their boots echoed in awkward rhythms between the banks of metal lockers. Abner looked around. "Years ago my old locker used to be along here somewhere."

Billy slowed.

Abner squinted with effort of recall, then stopped before number 116. "This one."

"So what's the combination?" Billy said. He was trying to make a small joke. Anything to ease the tension.

Abner raised a dark eyebrow at his son, then squinted with thought. Suddenly he spun the dial right, left, right—and lifted the latch.

"Geez, Pa!"

"I'm not dumb," his father said, looking straight at him.

Billy met his gaze. "I know that, Pa. And nobody

ever said you were."

Abner walked on, and Billy followed.

Outside on the steps, Abner looked toward Main Street. "Tenth grade was my last year. I knew it was going to be the end of high school for me. That's why I remember it so well."

Billy nodded.

His father turned back to survey the school, its tall front, its blank windows. "Dragging myself around on crutches, being a cripple, that's what changed me, I guess. Then Robert . . ."

Their eyes met. Billy said, "We got some time before milking. You want to go uptown and get a doughnut or something?"

After a pause Abner said, "All right. Sure."

In the bakery they took a table where they both could see out. They ate their sugar doughnuts and sipped their coffee. They didn't talk. In the middle of this, Mark Kenwood and King appeared on the opposite side of the street, walking along in silence as well; Billy and Abner paused to watch them.

The Kenwoods stopped to look in the window of Kovach's Sports and Tackle store. Mark Kenwood pointed; King shrugged, and then they went inside.

"King must need some new equipment," Abner remarked.

Billy returned to his doughnut but felt Abner's eyes.

"You know one reason why I'm glad that you play baseball?"

Billy was silent.

"Because baseball is the only way we can beat someone like King Kenwood."

"What do you mean, 'we'?" Billy asked immediately.

"I mean us farm folks. Poor folks. You can include colored people in that—in general the lower classes. The ball field is the only place where they can compete with rich people. Off the field everything is rigged."

"I don't know if I entirely believe that, Pa," Billy said quietly.

Abner stared at Billy. "Well, you'll just have to find out for yourself, then, won't you?"

"Exactly," Billy said.

Abner blinked. Then he gave the smallest nod of understanding, and a trace of a smile.

"So anyway," Abner said, leaning back, sipping his coffee as he glanced across the street, "I suppose we could get Big Danny to help with chores during the school week. Though he'd have to live in."

"He could stay in Robert's room," Billy said. "We wouldn't have to change much, just make a place for him to sleep."

"We'll ask your mother," Abner said. "Get her opinion on that."

Billy nodded.

"And about the car," Abner continued, "if you want to help me pull the engine and transmission, we can see about getting that Chevy back on the road."

"We'll do it this weekend," Billy said with enthusiasm.

"We can at least start," Abner said. "It's a big job. You can't rush a job like that."

That night during supper Abner himself brought up the plan for having Big Danny live in during the week and help with the chores. "Though he'd have to stay in Robert's room," Abner said.

After a moment's hesitation, Mavis said, "There's no reason why he can't. I'll call his father, and we can go get him tonight."

"With Danny here there's going to be more cooking and cleaning for your mother," Abner said sternly, turning to Billy. "So I want you to give her a hand once in a while."

"No problem," Billy said.

"Starting tonight, with dishes," Mavis said. She smiled.

Abner bent over his plate. "Also, Billy and I are going to take a look at the Chevy," he mumbled. "See if there's anything there worth fixing."

Mavis this time had no words; her eyes suddenly glistened.

"Got to teach Billy a thing or two about cars," Abner said with a shrug, "so as he doesn't have to depend on the crooked mechanics of the world."

In the morning Billy jerked awake to the sound of an alarm clock in Robert's room. Then Big Danny's feet thudded to the floor. Billy let out a breath, though his heart pounded on loudly for a few seconds. He lay there, listening to Big Danny move about. Noises from Robert's room made the house feel whole again.

After Danny went downstairs, after the screen door slammed, Billy turned over and snuggled deeper into his blankets. For the first time in years he could go back to sleep. He lay there, eyes open in the darkness. After ten minutes of tossing and turning he got up and switched on the light. He went to his closet. There he removed his new school clothes and laid the slacks, the madras shirt, the penny loafers on his bed. He stepped back to survey them; he tried them on. All together, they still didn't feel right. He still felt strange in them. So he took his time and tried on various combinations of new and older clothes.

In the end he decided on the madras shirt, his comfortable old blue jeans, plus the penny loafers. The shirt felt fresh and bright, and the new shoes light on his feet. Dressed for school, he combed his hair and inspected himself in the small mirror. His metal teeth still gleamed, and he had a new pimple on his chin, but this morning none of that bothered him.

Appearing downstairs, he waited for his mother to be surprised by his new look. But Mavis was too smart for that. "Good morning," was all she said as she bustled about with breakfast.

"What do you think, Ma?" Billy finally said, turning in place.

"You look fine," she said. "Now sit down and eat."

"You know, Ma?" he said as he chewed. "I think

if I studied some, I could actually get a B in English."

"Eat your pancakes, dear, or you'll miss the bus."

As Billy headed down the driveway, he paused twice to shine his shoes, first right, then left, on the backs of the legs of his jeans, then ambled on. At the road he turned to look back at the farm. His mother remained on the porch; she had been watching him the whole way. He waved to her, and she waved back. Then his eyes went to the rest of the farm, which this morning looked smaller. Maybe it was the sky, particularly high and blue today, but if he squinted his eyes, the place was almost like a toy farm—tiny tractors and barns and house and silo. He had a sudden sensation that he could move the buildings about, fix them, change them, just by reaching out his hands.

A clear, sharp call of a meadowlark brought him back to reality. When he turned back to the road, he found his bus just arriving. For the first time in his life he felt like he might be going somewhere.

WILL WEAVER teaches English and creative writing at Bemidji State University. He has written two books for adults, *Red Earth, White Earth* and *Gravestone Made of Wheat*, and is the winner of both the McKnight and the Bush foundations' prizes for fiction. His first two books for young adults, *Striking Out*, a 1994 Best Book for Young Adults (ALA), and *Farm Team*, a 1996 Best Book for Young Adults (ALA) and winner of the 1996 IRA Distinguished Book Award for Young Adults, are also about Billy Baggs.

Will Weaver lives in Bemidji, Minnesota, with his wife and two children.